Lord Calne's Christmas Ruby

Jude Knight

I0586853

Published by Jude Knight
Copyright 2017 Judith Anne Knighton writing as Jude Knight

ISBN: 978-0-9951049-2-1

TITCHFIELD PRESS

Dedication

To the man who thinks my value is above rubies. I have loved you all my adult life, since ten days after my nineteenth birthday. Forty-eight years and counting. The value you place in me, the respect you give me, has made me who I am. Thank you.

Chapter One

Philip Daventry escorted yet another vapid debutante back to her Mama, who coyly remarked that dear Amanda had never been so pleased with a dance, and another would not be beyond the bounds of propriety. "Dear Amanda" giggled and nodded, but not without an anxious look at Philip's twisted hand, the scarring hidden by the glove but the deformity in no way concealed.

Philip made the excuse he was promised for the rest of the evening, and must, even now, find his next partner. Before he could extract himself, the mother declared both ladies would be at home to the newly minted Earl of Calne whenever he cared to call. "Amanda so enjoys a drive in the park, Lord Calne," she hinted, broadly.

Philip, who lacked a carriage, horses, and the inclination to give Miss Amanda any encouragement, pretended he had not understood, merely bowing and taking his leave.

Now he would need to either seek an introduction to another partner, or hide so he was not caught in his untruth.

The evening's hostess, the Duchess of Haverford, was nowhere to be seen among the crush she called, "just a gathering of friends with perhaps a little impromptu dancing or a game of cards; nothing so formal as a ball."

Or so his uncle reported, when he insisted Philip attend. "Your man of business is right, Philip. You need to marry money if you're to save what remains of the estate. No need for it to be a cold business affair. Men have fallen in love with heiresses before now. At least come with me this evening, and see if there is anyone you might be able to warm to."

Philip had allowed himself to be persuaded, but without much hope. He had been right. Every one to whom the duchess presented him simpered and tittered, and openly displayed their willingness to accept the position of Countess of Calne, while unsuccessfully hiding their distaste for his deformity. Their mothers or aunts or older sisters ignored the hand entirely, which was somehow worse, since their only interest in him was to show off the paces of their particular maiden with the enthusiasm of a fairground horse dealer and, he rather thought, with as much veracity.

The evening was an off-season event. By far the largest part of the *ton* was already off on some country estate, enjoying the peace of early winter or the bustle and drama of a house party. Thank goodness. At least the experience had taught him the folly of breaking cover in the height of the Season, to be hunted by an even larger pack of matchmaking mothers.

If he couldn't find the duchess, perhaps Uncle Henry would introduce him to a suitable partner. His uncle had made himself scarce as soon as he had handed Philip over to the duchess. No doubt he had found some friends with whom to play cards or talk about politics and the war. Philip should have turned back when Uncle Henry admitted, in the carriage, that without his daughter to run interference, he would avoid the main dancing rooms and thus the snares and pitfalls of those who felt his widower status made him fair game. And Uncle Henry was thirty-five years Philip's senior and not an earl, but merely the fourth son of one; a career officer with the Horse Guard.

Mind you, Uncle Henry was neither crippled nor all but destitute, conditions which must count against Philip. He'd ordered everything marketable in his inheritance to be sold, but the earldom would still be in debt when the accounting was complete.

While he had been pondering his sorrows, Philip had skirted the dancing floor, still without seeing the duchess or Uncle Henry, and the sets had formed for the next dance. Perhaps he would find the card room, and stay with Uncle Henry until it was time for the appointed dance. After which, he was leaving. This whole evening had been a mistake.

A long hall with doors on either side led from the ballroom. He strode along, having learned earlier in the evening that strolling was an invitation to acquire a twittering female on either arm. Nodding politely as he passed those he recognised, he glanced in each room with an open door. A retiring room with chaperones drinking tea or ratafia, a group listening to a singer, two closed doors in a row and then a room set up with tables, and intent groups of two or four or six playing cards.

Philip stood for a moment just inside the door, until the nearest group asked if he would like to join them. But Uncle Henry wasn't in the room, so he declined politely and went back to his search.

The next room was dark. The one after was lit, the door partly open, though not enough to see into the room. Women's voices indicated the room was in use, and he paused to listen. He would not intrude on a private conversation.

"Really, Miss Finchurch, I cannot imagine what Lady Carngrove is thinking, bringing you here to mingle with your betters."

Another voice; a vicious purr somehow familiar to Philip. "Perhaps she imagines the perfume of Miss Finchurch's wealth will overcome the stench of her origins?"

Definitely not the card room. Harpies of this stamp would not attack so openly in front of an audience, and Uncle Henry would not stand by while they did. Philip should do something. While he hesitated, those inside continued to talk.

"I do not believe so, girls. Lady Carngrove intends all that lovely money for her darling Ceddie. As if he would even consider such a thing! Why, Miss Finchurch is quite old!"

The next voice was crisp, but with a bubble of a laugh running through it. "My goodness, I must really worry you, for you to descend to such a puerile level of nursery bullying."

Philip grinned. The victim was not entirely helpless then.

Before the babble of rejoinders sorted themselves out, he pushed the door open. "Miss Finchurch? Ah, there you are." It was a small reading room, lined with bookshelves and with comfortable chairs grouped around low tables, just the right height for a drink and a book.

The target of the others' spite was clearly the one at bay, seated by the fire with an open book on her lap. She turned her face to him an instant before the others. Old? True, she was not a girl fresh from the schoolroom, but rather a lady in her mid-twenties, unlined face a perfect oval, with large brown eyes under arched brows, a tilt-tipped nose, and a quantity of light brown hair pulled up into a confection of hair atop her head, a few strands pulled loose to frame the delightful whole.

She met his smile with a quizzical tip of the head, and he ignored the five ladies standing over her. "Our dance is in a few minutes, Miss Finchurch, so I came to find you. Would you care to take a short stroll while we wait?"

Would she take the rescue, he wondered, glancing from her to the others? Three were strangers. One, he vaguely recognised. But the remaining woman… He nodded a polite but cold acknowledgement to Lady Markhurst, who had pretended to accept his courtship when he was last in Society four years ago, after recovering from the injuries that ended his army career and brought him home to England.

Lady Markhurst had soon made it clear his only attraction was his unwed cousins, one an earl and one the heir to an earl. Philip wasn't close to either, and had not seen her since she discovered that fact. He assumed her pursuit was unsuccessful; certainly, she had wed before the end of that season, to a lowly and rather elderly baron who proved to be not as wealthy as rumour had painted.

Clearly, Philip's attractiveness had increased with his accession to the title, since Lady Markhurst fluttered her fan and her eyelashes, and fingered the diamond drop dangling from her ornate necklace into the valley between her breasts. "Why, Lord Calne. Surely you cannot intend to dance with a merchant's daughter. Your inheritance cannot be in such a dire state as that. Let me save you from such a fate by offering myself as a partner instead." The throaty note in her last sentence made it a naughty innuendo.

He ignored Lady Markhurst and her outstretched hand, offering Miss Finchurch his bad arm, which functioned well enough as a prop for a lady. Lady Markhurst's face flushed and then whitened. She had not learned to control her temper, then.

Miss Finchurch made up her mind, set her book to one side, and stood to slip her hand into his elbow, and he turned to the door. Lady Markhurst launched another attack before they reached it.

"Do be warned, Miss Finchurch. The Calne title comes with a bankrupt estate and a crippled earl."

Miss Finchurch gripped his arm, making him wince, and she sensed it, too, the fires she was about to turn on Lady Markhurst doused by her concern for him. He took another step towards the door.

"Ignore Lady Markhurst, Miss Finchurch. I would say her disappointment in her ambitions has made her bitter, but she was always a scold."

His mother would have punished such rudeness, but he was well compensated by the gasps from behind him as he whisked Miss Finchurch into the hall and pulled the door closed. She was tiny; perhaps no more than five feet tall, the top of her head barely on a level with his shoulder, and he shortened his steps when he realised she was near running to keep up with him. She was, however, by no means quelled. "You and Lady Markhurst are old friends, it seems, Lord Calne."

"Not since I discovered her heart was made of the same substance as the stones in her necklace."

Miss Finchurch laughed, an amused gurgle. "Paste, you mean? Very appropriate! Cold, hard and false."

"Paste? Really?"

"I am the daughter and niece of diamond merchants, Lord Calne. I would need to examine the smaller stones more closely, but the drop is decidedly not a diamond. Perhaps it is ill bred of me to disclose the lady's secrets, so I shall compound the error by making it clear I am not looking for a husband, and if I were, I would not accept a fortune hunter under any circumstances."

A game of truths, was it? "Nor am I looking for a wife, Miss Finchurch. Especially one prepared to take a destitute cripple for the sake of his useless title. But a dance might be safe enough? I have managed several tonight and am as yet unwed."

That earned him the gurgle again, and they took the positions for a long dance, Philip apologising in advance for being unable to grasp with his withered left hand.

Miss Finchurch assured him she would grasp well enough for them both. "What happened, Lord Calne? Or were you born with it? Or should I not ask?"

How refreshing to meet someone who said outright what everyone else speculated about in whispers behind his back. Philip answered as simply. "I was in the wrong place at the wrong time. We were crossing a newly repaired bridge in Sicily. But the French had set dynamite, and it blew up, with half the baggage train. I lost the use of one hand." His writing hand, but he could manage well enough with his right, after years of tutors who had punished the use of the other. "Many lost more." His brother-in-law for one, which directly led to the deaths of his sister and her baby. She had gone into labour shortly after the news reached her in Malta, and when the child was born dead, she had turned her face to the wall and died. Or so Philip had been told when he recovered from the fever, by which time he was in England, in his uncle's care.

"You were in the army?"

"With the Engineers." And in charge of the repair of the bridge. He should have detected the sabotage. The deaths—all the deaths, not just those of his family—were his fault.

Their turn came in the figures of the dance, giving him time to bludgeon his mind into accepting that the room was not caving in on him; that the glittering crowd were not about to turn on him to demand his immediate conviction for dereliction of duty.

Either something in his face caused Miss Finchurch to take pity on him, or she was bored with the subject, because when they stood out next, she reopened the conversation by asking whether he enjoyed this kind of entertainment in a voice so doubtful he laughed.

"No more than you, I suspect, Miss Finchurch, though more so since fate handed me a partner who does not send me to sleep with talk of fashion and gossip. Tell me, what is a diamond assessor doing in a Haverford House entertainment? You came with Lady Carngrove, those vixens said?"

"My aunt." The mournful tone suggested this was not a circumstance for congratulation. "I live with her. At the moment."

He sensed tragedy and, come to think of it, she had referred to her father and uncle in the past tense. But she did not wear black, which hinted her bereavement was not recent. He was uncertain whether to express his commiserations.

"I lived in India until eighteen months ago. My parents died there when I was a child, and my uncle raised me. When he died, I returned to England, and to my mother's sister. And thus, you have my whole history, my lord."

"I grew up in various ports around the globe," he offered in return. "My father was a naval officer, and my mother took me and my sister in his wake. I was intended for the navy myself, but I…" He had been about to tell her about his terrible *mal de mer*, which was not something he disclosed to anyone if he could help it. "I discovered I loved designing and making things: useful things like roads and canals and bridges. So, I trained as an engineer at the Royal Military Academy, and there you have my history."

"Ah," Miss Finchurch reminded him, "but I brought mine up to date. You neglected the small matter of your title. Did you always know you were to be an earl?"

"Not at all. My father was a younger son, and I barely knew my uncle and cousins. The earldom was safe in their line, with an heir and his younger brother, and the heir betrothed. It would be yet if the two cousins had had the sense not to travel together in a racing carriage through a forest in a storm, several weeks after their father died. The lawyers had the dev-- a difficult job finding me, because the last address my uncle had for my father was before he died, and that was eight years ago, and in South Africa." They'd been surprised to find their lost heir in the north-west England, working on an aqueduct for a canal. But not as surprised as Philip had been to find he was now the Earl of Calne.

Miss Finchurch raised her brows, and her eyes smiled if her lips didn't. "I feel you would prefer commiserations on your new title rather than congratulations."

He did not bother to suppress his bark of laughter. "You are correct," he told her, "and the sooner I can get back to my real work the better." Winter had put a stop to canal building, or he'd be there now. Still, meeting Miss Finchurch had made the evening bearable, and would be one of the pleasanter memories of his expedition into the foreign landscape of high Society.

"What is your real work, my lord?"

Philip needed no more encouragement to give her a quick overview of the canal, and especially the aqueduct that would take it across a valley to join with the Bridgewater. At least, he had intended a quick overview. But her intelligent questions lured him into a far deeper discussion, which they continued when the music ended, strolling through the rooms to avoid being caught up in any other group. When a lady who must be her aunt retrieved Miss Finchurch, shooting Philip a resentful glare, he let her go with real reluctance.

What a lovely woman Miss Finchurch was, and what a pity he was too poor to think of pursuing the acquaintance.

Chapter Two

"You need not think of Calne, Margaret," Aunt Cecilia told Lalamani Finchurch in the carriage on the way home. "The whole *ton* knows he has not a feather to fly with. But your uncle will not consider him for you, even though you are an heiress, and the best such a poor specimen of a man might hope for. You are to wed Cecil as soon as he is of age."

Lalamani didn't comment. No point in reminding Aunt Cecilia that she used her second name, not her first. Nor would she say Lord Calne had offered no flattery nor promised to visit, but had instead discussed aqueducts and canals, those he had built and those he planned to build. She would certainly not argue that Calne was a fine, fit, elegant man whose withered hand did not disable him, his enthusiasm and intelligence far more to her taste than the lazy and effete gentlemen who flattered her out of one side of their mouths while sneering from the other. Above all, she would not point out she was twenty-three, nearly twenty-four, and neither her marriage nor her fortune were under her uncle's control.

Aunt Cecilia would have ignored any remark she made as irrelevant, since Aunt Cecilia believed the world would march to her order if she only charged on in her chosen direction. She ignored any facts that did not fit her preconceptions, including her own son's opposition to marriage with his older cousin, the five years between his age and hers seeming an insuperable barrier to an eighteen-year-old.

Cecil's guardian, his father's uncle, had forbidden the match while Cecil was so young but, despite this, in Aunt Cecilia's mind the matter was certain. She nonetheless kept a careful watch for possible poachers in her son's preserves.

It didn't matter. This was the last *ton* party Lalamani would attend, if all went as planned in the morning. She and Cecil had decided. Or, rather, Lalamani had made up her mind, and Cecil had cooperated, since it fitted with his own desires.

Tomorrow, they would leave together, and disappear. Cecil was heading north to a hunting lodge with friends. Lalamani had received a friendly letter from her father's sister, the widow of a country rector who still lived in the village she and her husband had served for forty years. Lalamani had grown up with letters from Aunt Hannah, and couldn't believe she hadn't thought of going there before now.

This morning, Cecil had escorted her to her man of business, who was also her trustee, to collect this quarter's pin money. Tomorrow, he would see her to the coaching inn, and onto the coach for her aunt's village. She would visit, and if all went well, she would take refuge with Aunt Hannah until her twenty-fifth birthday, when she had control of her own fortune.

With luck, Aunt Cecilia would assume she and Cecil had eloped and would keep their absence a secret so her brother-in-law did not come running to stop his ward's marriage.

With even more luck, her first inkling Cecil and Lalamani had gone in different directions would be when Cecil returned from his hunting trip in the new year. Time enough for Lalamani to find out whether she wanted to stay with Aunt Hannah, and whether Aunt Hannah would want her to stay. She could deal with Aunt Cecilia easily enough if only she had a safe place to wait out the next year.

Chapter Three

Lalamani, waking in the little room she had been
assigned when she arrived in Feldon Roding late the
previous evening, looked around it without
pleasure. The walls were covered in a faded print
that must have been a dull puce when it was first
put up and was now an indeterminate beige, almost
the same colour as the painted ceiling. Its trim had
once, perhaps, been gold but was now a rather dirty
brown. The walls were panelled to chair-rail height
in a dark wood made dull by unknown years of
poorly applied polish. The drab curtains added to
the overall impression of being in a muddy hole
underground.

"What colour would you call those curtains,
Milly?" she asked when her maid arrived with a jug
of hot water and a warning her Aunt, Mrs Thorpe,
always rose to break her fast in the downstairs
dining room, and Miss Lalamani had better look
sharp if she wanted to join her.

Milly looked doubtfully at the curtains.
"Chocolate?"

"I was thinking mud," Lalamani said. "The yellow sprigged, Milly. I feel the need of something cheerful."

Milly put the pink gingham back on the hooks and lifted down the dress Lalamani selected. The muted pink, which Lalamani had always rather liked, today looked almost the same shade as the wall it hung on.

Dressed, Lalamani went down through a stairwell and hall of the same faded, depressing hues to a dining room that might have been rather fine fifteen years ago, had it been decorated in more appealing colours and had the black crepe swags draped along every available surface been folded away, or at least shaken out and dusted.

Aunt Hannah was helping herself to a heaping plate of food. Lalamani noted the food, at least, was not depressing. Aunt Hannah clearly believed in starting the day with variety and quality.

"Lalamani, my dear, how lovely you look, and how you brighten up this sad old house." Aunt Hannah dabbed at the tears that overflowed from her pale blue eyes.

The house was, Lalamani had to agree, rather sad, with its drab colours and mourning swags. Aunt Hannah, too, was swathed in deep black though her husband the rector had been gone for nearly nine years.

"Have some bacon, Lalamani, dear. And eggs? How do you like your eggs?" Aunt Hannah fussed over making sure Lalamani had a loaded plate, clucking anxiously that Lalamani must say if anything was lacking and Aunt Hannah would order it for the morrow.

"I am very pleased to see you, Lalamani, of course. Dear Hadley's little girl." Aunt Hannah leaned over the table to pat Lalamani's hand, her eyes watering slightly. "I do not know when I last had company. And is your aunt, Lady Carngrove, well? And little Lord Carngrove?"

"Yes, very well," Lalamani said. "They are both well." How Cedric would frown to be referred to as little Lord Carngrove, as if he was still in leading strings.

Aunt Hannah's face glowed with the warmth of her smile. "They will miss you, I am certain. But how kind of them to spare you to me for Christmas."

"I am very happy to be here, Aunt Hannah."

"It is lovely to have you here. I could not be more pleased, Lalamani, but…" The anxious expression that seemed habitual deepened to a frown. "I do not know, my dear, how I shall keep you entertained. I live very quietly, you know."

"I am here to visit you, Aunt Hannah. I am happy to keep you company, and perhaps I can help with your visiting and your parish work?" Lalamani had long been fascinated by the many activities Aunt Hannah had written about over the years.

"Oh, my dear, I do not do much anymore." The faded cheeks turned pink, and the ready tears brimmed over again. "I know I said in my letters… It was wrong of me. One should never tell falsehoods, but truly I did do all those things. Just not since the new rector… His sister, you know.

She is quite right, quite right. It is her place to…
And I would not want to… I truly would not, my
dear. I feel so old and useless, and when I wrote to
you, I could pretend, for just a while…"

Her voice faded away as tears sleeted down her
cheeks. Lalamani patted her on the arm, wondering
somewhat desperately what to do next. This was
completely outside of Lalamani's experience. Her
life had not provided a plethora of weeping elderly
widows.

"Dear Aunt Hannah, of course you pretended.
Anyone would have done the same. There was no
harm in it. Oh, Aunt Hannah, please do not cry."

After several minutes of patting and
reassurances, Aunt Hannah visibly pulled herself
together and gave Lalamani a watery smile. "There,
you will be running away when you have barely
arrived. I am so sorry to be such a watering pot, my
dear. Come, try some of this lovely bacon. I must
say the parish people are so good to me. I never
want for food for my plate. I really do not. Why
Mrs Wright brought me this lovely cut of bacon just
yesterday morning…"

She carried on while Lalamani ate, enumerating
all the givers of the food they enjoyed. The tea,
brought by the servant who had opened the door to
Lalamani and Milly the night before, was not up to
the same standard; it was weak and of an
indeterminate flavour between milky water and,
Lalamani thought, dishwater.

Aunt Hannah, after taking a sip, looked with
consternation at the servant, a small bent elderly

lady in the same faded black as she herself wore. "Oh dear, Addy. It is worse than I remembered."

"I told you, madam. Gave you the floor sweepings, I shouldn't wonder."

"Addy! No uncharitable remarks, if you please. As if they would. It is very kind of Dr Wagley and his sister. Lalamani, the rector and his sister give us a canister of tea every Christmas. A whole canister! Is that not generous?" She looked doubtfully at the cup.

Lalamani exchanged glances with the servant and resolved to have a private conversation with her very soon.

Something was wrong here. Uncle Herbert had bought Aunt Hannah a house when her husband died, and set up a trust to provide her with an income. She should not be dependent for her very food on the generosity of her departed husband's former parishioners.

Everything Lalamani had seen in the house was faded, dismal, and much mended, from the furnishings to the clothes Aunt Hannah and her servant Addy wore. Yes, and not too clean. Surely a house of this size needed more than one servant? But Addy, bustling out and then back again with a pot of peppermint tisane to replace the undrinkable China tea, was the only one Lalamani had seen, and far too old to manage all the work on her own.

Lalamani and Milly would have to help. Ladies' maids generally held themselves above housework, but Milly was an agreeable girl, and would probably consent to work alongside Lalamani to make the place more comfortable for Aunt Hannah and her woman, especially if Lalamani paid Milly extra to assuage the loss of dignity.

Yes. Dealing with the dirty corners would be simple enough. Finding out the cause of Aunt Hannah's unexpected poverty was unlikely to be as easy.

Chapter Four

Philip had been warned. But he found Highwood Hall in an even worse state than he expected. "The house in Feldon Roding has been the main seat of the Calnes for hundreds of years," the lawyer had said, "but your uncle hasn't lived there for fifteen years, or kept it staffed for ten. And he refused to allow money to be spent on repairs. I understand the roof has failed in places, in the main house and in the outbuildings."

The entire west wing had failed, the roof collapsed into the crumbling walls that were all that remained. The centre block was still largely intact, but the east wing was going the way of its counterpart, with gaping holes instead of tiles and the rafters showing through.

The stables were in no better case. Philip tethered his borrowed horse where it could reach water and grass, and poked around as best he could without risking life and limb. He'd hoped to be able to do some repairs in order to increase the possible sale price, but razing the place to the ground might be the best use of his meagre savings.

One thing was certain. He would not be staying in his own house tonight. He'd better get settled at the local inn and walk back later, to make a start on a proper assessment.

A day with her aunt only deepened Lalamani's concerns.

Adidiah—Addy—was happy to express an opinion, as she and Lalamani scrubbed the kitchen floor. "It's a crying shame, Miss Lalamani. Mrs Thorpe don't have but a pittance for herself. If not for the people roundabouts, why, she'd starve."

"But, Addy, she has an income. She could even sell this house and move into a smaller place if she needed to."

"Is that a fact, Miss Lalamani? Rector, he gives her a bit of money now and then. Don't know about no income, though. I never heard of such."

Lalamani wasn't sure of the details of the trust; it had been set up before she began acting as her uncle's secretary. But her uncle loved his sister, and he was a wealthy man. Why, the house itself attested to his generosity; shabby though it was, it was large, well built, and had lovely proportions.

An interview with her aunt was in order, and afterwards, perhaps a letter to Lalamani's lawyer who had served her uncle well over many years.

"Aunt Hannah," Lalamani began as they took a break from housework that afternoon to walk the two miles to the village, "it is impertinent of me, I know, but I am concerned about you."

"You do not need to be, dear Lalamani." Aunt Hannah's eyes watered again. "I have all I need. Everyone is so generous to me." A shadow crossed over her face. "I do wish, though, I was able to pay my dear Addy. I worry about her, dear, I do indeed. If anything should happen to me… Well, I must just pray about it and trust God would look after her."

"Aunt Hannah," she tried again, "what happened to the money Uncle Herbert left you?"

She stopped in her tracks and peered at Lalamani, her pale blue eyes bewildered. "Money, dear? He paid for the house; the man from London came and found it for me. That was so lovely of Herbert, sweetheart. Though I could wish it was closer to the village, but Miss Wagley—she's the rector's sister, dear—she told me it was better I put a bit of distance between myself and the village. The people needed to get used to calling on her, she said. And she was quite right, no doubt, but I do find it hard sometimes, my dear." She began walking again, shaking her head.

"But the money, Aunt Hannah," Lalamani reminded her.

"No one told me anything about any money, my dear. I was not very well, of course. Such a terrible ague. So many people died. My poor dear husband. The inn keeper. Twelve babies they told me, so sad, I always think, when a baby dies." Her eyes filled again.

Lalamani was becoming inured to the easy tears and carried on regardless. "I'm so sorry to make you think about that sad time, Aunt Hannah, but it is important. When did you hear about the house?" It must have taken some time for word of Uncle Thorpe's death to get to India and for Uncle Herbert to send back his instructions to his lawyer.

"Let me see, dear. Mr Thorpe took the ague in January. He was one of the first in the village. I nursed him, of course, and we thought he was rallying, but he died in early February. Too much strain on his heart, dear, the doctor said.

"So many sick people in the village and out on the farms. So sad, my dear, especially when it started in the foundlings' home. I did what I could, but I was so tired, and then I fell sick myself. If not for Addy, I would have died too, I expect.

"How mysterious are the ways of God, for me to be spared and not those little children. A useless old woman like me, living past her time." Paradoxically, Aunt Hannah seemed cheered rather than depressed by this and blew her nose enthusiastically on the handkerchief with which she had been dabbing her eyes.

"So, when did Uncle Herbert's lawyer come to see you about the house?" Lalamani asked.

"Oh, I never met him. He visited while I was sick. I had the ague again twice more that year, and he came the second time, in the summer it was. Indeed, by the time I was well enough to go about a bit again, they had already moved me into the house. I was so grateful, for I cannot deny the cottage they found for me when they moved me from the rectory was draughty, and the roof leaked. But there. I must not complain, and it was good of the people to find me a place.

"The new rector—he was the new rector then—came to see me and explained my brother had rented the house for me, though what I will do when the lease runs out I do not know, my dear.

"And he said the parish would look after me, since I had no income. And they have, Lalamani. Why, Dr Wagley even gives me money from time to time. One does need money, unfortunately. At last quarter day, he gave me a whole ten pounds! Think of that. Ten pounds."

The lease? The house was Aunt Hannah's free and clear. And ten pounds? Lalamani had spent much more on a walking dress.

They'd arrived in the village, and Lalamani dropped the topic for the moment, but she would be seeking an introduction to this Dr Wagley without delay!

Miss Finchurch was the first person Philip saw as he rode into the village. At first, he did not believe it, since he had been seeing her in every short comely woman he passed for days. But there she was, her face turned his way as she talked to the elderly woman beside her.

She wasn't aware of him, her focus all on her companion. He noted the shop she entered, a village general store. Should he follow immediately, or take a room at the inn first and look her up after? The hired horse was tired. He should hand it over to the care of the grooms. He nudged it on into the inn-yard and dismounted with his usual care, pleased the damned hand managed to maintain hold on the reins. It ached a bit, but his exercises had helped him to gain and keep some measure of function.

A walk would do him good. He gave his saddle bags to the innkeeper with instructions to prepare a room, and headed out to find Miss Finchurch.

She was still in the shop. He knew her by her lack of height, and by some indefinable knowledge of her shape and the way she moved, though her face was hidden by her bonnet and she was half hidden on the other side of a stack of shelves.

"Oh dear," the elderly woman was saying, "Lalamani, my love, are you sure? Can you afford it? I should not wish you to spend your money on me."

Lalamani. What an unusual name. Beautiful and exotic, and somehow precisely right for the lady whose memory had haunted him for days.

"And why not, may I ask?" Lalamani replied firmly. "Who else should I spend it on than the aunt who was like a mother to my papa? Why, it is my Christian duty, Aunt Hannah."

Philip rounded the shelves and was gratified by Miss Finchurch's expression of surprised delight before she schooled her face to gracious welcome.

"My lord! What a surprise to see you here! Aunt Hannah, may I make known to you Lord…?"

Philip interrupted, holding out a hand to the lady. "Lord Calne's engineer, Philip Daventry, madam, at your service."

Miss Finchurch's eyes narrowed, but she did not betray his prevarication. "My aunt, Mrs Thorpe."

Mrs Thorpe held out a wrinkled hand for him to salute. "Mr Daventry? Oh my goodness. I suppose you have come to see to the Hall. Daventry is the earl's family name, of course, so you must be some kind of cousin. Does the earl wish the Hall repaired? But I cannot think it is fit for anyone to stay in. Certainly, no one has stayed there this past thirty years. More! You will stay with us, of course. Only, Lalamani," and here she dropped her voice to what she clearly imagined was a whisper, "I'm not perfectly sure we have another whole set of sheets!"

"I have a room at the inn, Mrs Thorpe, but thank you for the offer."

Mrs Thorpe looked relieved, but insisted, "But you will visit. You must. You have come all this way. And you are a friend of my niece's."

"I expect Mr Daventry is as surprised to see me as I am to see him," Miss Finchurch said.

Philip hazarded his luck. "Yes, but I am always happy to see a friend, Miss Finchurch, and feel very fortunate my duties brought me to the same village you were visiting. I had not hoped to see you again so soon." Or at all, though he had thought about her more often than he should, given his lack of a decent future to offer her.

Her slight frown was doubtful, but she refrained from commenting, and Mrs Thorpe filled the awkwardness of her silence by declaring she would ask the shop assistant to cut off twenty yards, if dear Lalamani was absolutely certain it would not be too expensive.

Receiving Miss Finchurch's assurance, she bustled off to make her purchases, leaving Philip to make his explanations. He took the high ground by speaking first. "Thank you for not exposing my title,

Miss Finchurch. I hope to avoid the village either toadying to me because I'm the earl, or pursuing me with duns because my predecessors owed them money. And I really am here as an engineer."

Her face cleared and she laughed. "I cannot blame you, and will support your deception, Mr Daventry. Do you make a long stay? I thought you would be back to your aqueduct."

"I hope to be able to return once the weather is settled enough for the work to start again, but meanwhile I can use the time to find out what repairs the Hall needs. And you? I did not know you planned a visit to Feldon Roding."

Miss Finchurch's eyes sparkled and her lips curved beguilingly, but she did not speak whatever mischief had amused her, saying only, "My Aunt Hannah has lived here for fifty years, and has often written to me about the village. I expect to enjoy my stay, although..." She trailed off, her smile turning to a frown.

"Although?" he prompted, when it became clear she was not going to continue that sentence, but she just sent him another bright smile.

"Aunt Hannah is ready," she said. "It has been lovely meeting you again, Mr Daventry."

He followed her to the counter, and swooped on the large parcel before she could add it to her own load, tucking it under his less functional arm so he could reach for her basket with the useful one. "Please allow me to carry your parcels to your carriage," he begged, to the amusement of both ladies.

"We are walking, Mr Daventry, and would not wish to take you out of your way."

"On the contrary," he rallied, "a walk is just what I need."

Once he knew which direction they were walking, Lord Calne assured Lalamani and her aunt the house was barely out of his way at all, being a mere five minutes beyond the turnoff to the Hall.

Lalamani suggested he could surrender his load when they reached the half-collapsed tangle of wrought-iron that had once controlled access to the Hall's main carriage way, but now merely wilted against the brick pillars on either side. Lord Calne insisted on escorting the ladies all the way home, and then accepted Aunt Hannah's offer of a cup of tea.

The arrival of a representative of an earl sent Addy into a brief panic. The parlour, she told Lalamani, was the proper place for such an august personage, but she and Milly had been clearing the other rooms to give them a thorough clean, and the parlour was now full of furniture, drapery, paintings, and ornaments.

But Lord Calne assured Addy he would prefer to have his tea in the kitchen, if she would be so kind, for then he would feel at home, and he had not had a home since his mother died. Which set both Addy and Aunt Hannah fussing over him to make him comfortable, and Lalamani was torn between gratitude at his swift intervention and exasperation at his skilful management of the two older women.

Yes, and Milly was a victim of his charm, too, sneaking peeks at him from the stool she reluctantly occupied after he insisted they all sit down, and blushing whenever he smiled in her direction.

The sooner he finished his cup of tea and his large helping of pound cake, the sooner he could take his leave and they could settle to their work, for Lalamani and Milly—with the enthusiastic support of Addy—were determined the whole house would be clean from the cellars to the attics before Christmas Eve.

Lord Calne accepted the second cup of tea Aunt Hannah offered, sipping it as he listened with every evidence of enjoyment to her stories of village life back when she was the rector's wife. She had a storyteller's gift for drama and pacing, and Lalamani was soon hanging on her words as much as she had when those stories arrived in letters. Gone was the anxious and diffident Aunt Hannah of today. As she talked about her life so long ago, her voice gained certainty and humour, her posture became confident, and Lalamani caught a glimpse of the warm, calm, loving rector's wife who had mothered the whole parish side-by-side with her beloved husband.

Lalamani was astounded when Milly began lighting candles and Lord Calne suddenly looked up at the window and said, "It is getting dark!"

"Oh dear," Aunt Hannah said, "I have kept you from your work."

"You are too kind to say I have been an importunate guest, far outstaying my welcome," Lord Calne replied. "But I beg you hold me excused, Mrs Thorpe. I was so absorbed in your stories I quite forgot myself."

"You must not neglect your work for the earl, Mr Daventry," Aunt Hannah scolded, and then cast a doubtful look outside.

"I will make an early start in the morning," Lord Calne promised, "but for now I had best make my way back to the inn while it is still light enough to see my way."

With a further exchange of mutual compliments, he disengaged himself from the kitchen and allowed Lalamani to usher him to the front of the house and out the door.

She locked the door behind him and slid the bolts, then rested her back against it, closing her eyes for a moment. For seven years, first in India and more recently in England, she had been courted and flattered by one man after another. She was not beautiful, and she was far too short, but she was passably pretty and, though merchant-born, she had the manners and training of a lady and her wealth covered a mountain of deficiencies. But none of her suitors tempted her to forgo her independence; none of them seemed to be aware of her mind or to care about engaging her in interesting conversation; not one could make her whole body tingle with just a smile.

Until now, she would have said, but Lord Calne was not a suitor. *He could be*, a treacherous voice whispered in the back of her mind. *He needs your money*. With a bit of encouragement… She shook her head but the thought would not be dislodged. What nonsense. As if she would want a husband she could purchase. As if Lord Calne would marry out of his class, even to save his estate. After all, heiresses were not unknown among the gentry, especially for a man as charming and kind as Lord Calne.

She pushed off from the door. *A lot of fuss about nothing.* Lord Calne would inspect his property tomorrow and then go back to London, and she would stay here and help her aunt. And the first step was to finish the cleaning.

Chapter Five

Three days of hard work saw a transformation of the main floor and the two occupied bed chambers. There was no disguising the shabbiness of the wall coverings and furnishings, but the ugly black swags were gone, bowls of holly leaves with their cheerful red berries brightened dust-free tables, and the woodwork gleamed.

Several times a day, their work was interrupted by visitors, locals who called to deliver gifts of food, examine the niece of their beloved 'Old Rector's wife', and gossip about the earl's man, who was spending every day at the broken-down old Hall.

"And not to hunt for treasure, like the last fellow," they agreed, for periodically the previous earl had sent outsiders to dig in the gardens or haul down walls, seeking something, and what could it be but a treasure. This man, though had hired several of the local men to work on the Hall with him, and he was focusing on salvage, not destruction.

"And right grateful for the work they are, Miss," one garrulous farm wife explained, "for with the enclosures and the taxes, it's hard enough to feed a family, especially at this time of year. Always some as starve afore the spring sowing. Not like when Old Rector was alive." She slid her eyes to Aunt Hannah and said no more.

Lalamani mentally measured what remained of her quarterly allowance against the cost of employing one or more of the locals. It had seemed a vast sum when she expected to pay only her own expenses and Milly's wages, and would certainly stretch to firewood for every room they had in use and other necessities for Aunt Hannah and Addy. But the two old ladies must have new garments, and her list of necessary repairs was growing room by room. Let alone refurbishment, though that might have to wait until after her twenty-fifth birthday. The house could be a very pleasant and comfortable place with a little work.

Aunt Hannah really needed a cook to take over the kitchen, a maid to assist with the housework, and someone to manage the garden and do necessary small repairs around the property. And a woman her age should not have to walk the two miles to the village, particularly on rainy days. But that would mean not just the cost of purchasing a gig and pony, and hiring someone to care for them, but also demolishing what had once been the stable and was now a pile of dangerous scrap, and building a new stable. Plus feed costs for both the animal and the stable hand.

Lalamani sighed, and started another list on a new page of her notebook.

Philip was also counting pennies. Most of his savings were invested up north with the consortium for whom he was building the aqueduct. Once he'd spent the absolute minimum needed to put what was left of the Calne holdings into marketable condition, he'd be left with a pittance until the canal started operating and earning.

He had hired local labour to help shore up sagging walls and make the roofs watertight over those parts of the buildings worth repairing. They were sullen to start with, and it didn't take him long to discover they were suspicious of anyone connected with the earl. "Old 'un never did anything good fer us'n," one of them said, as they began to relax around him. New 'un hasn't been next nor nigh the place since the old 'un died near a year ago. Stands to reason we don't expect much. Savin' your presence, sir."

Philip asked a few cautious questions, hoping to find out what had happened to the steward who vanished several years ago and the rents that hadn't been paid since. He got more than he bargained for.

As he worked alongside them on shoring up a wall or building a temporary shelter over a pile of recycled lumber, one man after another told him about the poverty resulting from the local enclosure act, pushed through several years earlier by large landowners such as the earl and rector. Smallholders had been left with too little land to farm, and most had left the area, abandoning properties that had been in their families for hundreds of years.

Two of his workmen proved to be his own tenants, barely able to farm the land they held from him because his absent predecessor had refused to make needed repairs and improvements for the past thirty years. The absconded steward had been a local man worn down from years of acting as a buffer between the local people and the earl, who drained resources and income from his unwanted property but never answered the steward's increasingly desperate appeals to put some money back in.

The men he had hired introduced him to others in the public room of the inn, and he spent his evening getting to know the local menfolk. Philip soon realised their expectations of the new earl might be low, but their hopes were high and had soared still higher on learning the earl had sent a man to repair the broken-down Hall.

"Stands to reason he plans to live here," one of the men argued, "And then he'll see for himself how things are, and will help us."

Philip soothed his increasing guilt with a silent promise to find a buyer who would want to spend most of the year in the village, and would look after his people. Those who were left.

Opinions on the rector were divided on class lines. The prosperous local farmers, crafters, and shopkeepers praised him as a man of faith, whose rousing sermons and firm management of the parish finances were a stark contrast to his predecessor. "Good man, the Reverend Thorpe, I'm not saying other," the innkeeper said. "But too soft on the poor. He'd give away the shirt on his back to a beggar would Old Rector Thorpe."

Under their breath and behind the backs of their betters, the poorer men painted a different picture: of a harsh zealot who showed one face to those who supported him and another to those he considered beneath his notice. Philip's disquiet increased at a casual reference to the quarterly rental owed to the earl and collected, since the steward left, by the local rector.

Chapter Six

On Sunday, Philip stood in the rear of the village church with other men he'd met during the week. "You could sit up there," one of them said, pointing to a box pew on the other side of the tall pulpit. "That's the Daventry pew, that is. And you're a Daventry, aren't you?"

Philip shook his head. "I'm more comfortable back here with you," he answered, though he promised himself a closer look later. Already, he'd noticed Daventry tombstones in the cemetery he'd passed on his way in, and Daventry memorials on the walls. Once, long ago, the Daventrys had valued this village and sent down deep roots. He could feel them tugging at a part of him he hadn't known existed. He had never belonged anywhere; had spent a lifetime roaming, first following his father from port to port, and later with the army.

"Home is not a place; it's people," his mother used to say. And with that his eye fell on Miss Finchurch, who was just entering the church with Mrs Thorpe, their maids behind them. The ladies made their way to the front of the nave, nodding and smiling at the gathered villagers as they passed.

Not long after they took their seats just under the pulpit, a man strode down the aisle, the academic robe he wore over his cassock billowing behind him. His identity was confirmed when he began to declaim the opening prayer, his congregation dutifully responding.

The service engaged only a fraction of Philip's attention. He watched the rest of the assembled villagers, and one bonneted head in particular, and let his mind drift to the conundrum of how to secure the future of the people of Feldon Roding while still meeting the debts he had inherited from his reckless uncle. Or, more properly, from his cousin, who had outlived his father and brother for four weeks before dying of his injuries.

The shouted word "Harlot!" jerked Philip's attention back to the rector, whose homily had begun while Philip was distracted. The rector, it transpired, had a low view of women, and was able to support his case with multiple passages from the Bible. Not just Proverbs chapter thirty-one, his ostensible text, where a mother warns her son against giving his strength to women, and against drunkenness. It was all one, the rector explained.

"For when a man allows himself to be blinded by lust, it is the woman who rules, and so it has been since the first woman sinned with the serpent and dragged all creation down into perdition."

He shot out a finger, and a woman in the gallery above him blanched as her neighbours pulled away. Another woman illustrated the story of Jezebel; a third, Delilah. David, whose lust for his general's wife led him to commit murder by enemy army, had his sins glossed over by the rector, who laid all the blame on Bathsheba. At least he had no candidate for Bathsheba in the congregation.

But the relief was short lived, because he found a Gomer, and a Potiphar's wife. Yes, and a Lot's wife, too. All, Philip noted, among the poorer members of the conversation, though at one point his gaze lingered on Miss Finchurch. Philip tensed, ready to leap to her defence, but the rector moved on to another victim. Which was probably just as well, since Philip could hardly challenge a man of the rector's age, and in a church, at that.

The rector was waiting in the doorway when they left the church, Aunt Hannah congratulated him on his homily, her voice doubtful. He narrowed his eyes at Lalamani. "My niece, Lalamani Finchurch, my brother Hadley's child. So lovely of her to visit. Lalamani, you have heard me speak of dear Reverend Wagley."

"A heathen name," the rector observed, sourly.

He was interrupted by the local squire and his wife, eager to meet Lalamani. Before she and her aunt had made their way to the gate, Lalamani had been introduced to most of the local gentry and the more prosperous farmers and tradespeople of the town, all of whom expressed their delight she'd come to keep her aunt company.

The squire's wife, Lady Picknell, was only the first to express her intention of making an afternoon call. "My son Arthur shall escort me this very afternoon," she said.

"My son would be delighted to meet you, Miss Finchurch, when he is home for Christmas," said another.

Lalamani suppressed a sigh. Perhaps Feldon Roding would not be the sanctuary from matchmaking mothers she'd longed for.

A few spots of rain, harbinger of a steadier downpour, sent those lingering in the churchyard scurrying for their homes or their carriages, and Lalamani put up the umbrella for their walk home. But when she and Aunt Hannah reached the gate, a voice called, "Mrs Thorpe!"

Lord Calne was holding the door open to the carriage from the inn, looking far more handsome than any man had a right to. "Quickly, ladies, come in out of the rain."

"But Milly and Addy—" Lalamani objected, planning to accept for her aunt and walk home with the maids herself. Anything to avoid being at close quarters with the pesky man, who had been invading her dreams, awake and asleep, since their waltz. Even more since his visit to the house days ago. Four days ago, and not a word since, which should be enough to prove he was not interested in furthering their acquaintance. And yet here he was.

"Your maids are already in the carriage," Lord Calne assured her. "Hop in, and I'll have you all home in the dry in no time."

"How thoughtful of you," Aunt Hannah said, as he propped the door open with his shoulder and offered her his good hand to help her up the carriage steps. With no alternative, Lalamani took his hand next. Even glove to glove, his touch sent a shiver through her, and she motioned to the maids to make room for her on the bench, leaving Lord Calne to sit next to Aunt Hannah.

"I feel sure," he said to Aunt Hannah, "that I remember my mother reading to me about some virtuous women in the Bible. Do you think we should inform the Reverend Wagley?"

Aunt Hannah suggested charitably the rector perhaps ran out of time to discuss the many heroines of Bible stories. Why, even Chapter 31 of Proverbs was primarily about the characteristics of a virtuous woman: the wife who was worth more than rubies, who managed a household, a family, a vineyard, and a textiles business.

"And Lalamani is a very pretty name, I think," she added, and then had to repeat what the Reverend had said at the gate. Philip agreed, and Lalamani found herself explaining it meant 'Ruby', in celebration of a spectacular trading deal her father and uncle had signed just before her birth, which set their enterprise on the road to success.

At the house, Aunt Hannah invited Philip to join them for lunch, and he sent the carriage back to the hall without him. Aunt Hannah was telling him all about the work they had been doing, "which is just as well, for we are to have visitors! Why, I believe half the village intends to call. They wish to meet Lalamani, of course. We shall be quite merry, and I am so grateful to my dear niece and her maid, for I do not mind telling you the heavy cleaning has been too much for me and poor Addy for some time."

Let him make what he would of Lalamani doing the cleaning. She was not ashamed of working with her hands to help her aunt. The smile he gave her seemed admiring, but she knew aristocrats demanded idleness from their wives and daughters. They could direct servants, but never sully their own fair hands. Well. She was no aristocrat, and she wouldn't pretend to a gentility she lacked. And as to the gentry of the village who had so neglected a woman who had served them for forty years, she would be polite for Aunt Hannah's sake, but she would certainly not pretend to them, either.

However, Lord Calne showed no signs of scorn, nor of objecting to once more eating in the kitchen with the maids. And when, as they were finishing their meal, Aunt Hannah and Addy began a low-voiced debate about what time to light the fire in the parlour for the expected guests, and which other rooms in the house could be left fireless until they could find someone willing to chop some of the wood in the woodshed into fire-sized pieces, he demanded to know the location of the axe.

"I will be back for visiting hour," he said, and set off to chop wood.

After an hour and a half, Lalamani went looking for him. The woodshed allowed for large pieces to be stored—drying—along one side and stacked chopped pieces on the other. The stack was at least triple its former size. Lord Calne, stripped to the waist, was at the chopping block in the centre of the shed, and she stood for a long moment admiring the width of his shoulders and the ripple of his muscles as he lifted a heavy mallet with his good arm and brought it down on a metal wedge inserted into the slice of trunk on the block.

The other arm was well muscled to the elbow, but the scarred forearm was markedly less robust than its counterpart, and his ungloved hand was twisted and deformed.

He brought the mallet down again, a mighty blow with all his weight behind it, and the trunk split, a chunk falling to the ground. He bent to pick it up, and his pantaloons tightened over his buttocks, riveting her eyes.

As Philip bent to pick up the bit of wood he'd knocked loose, he sensed Lalamani's presence and turned in time to see her admiring his anatomy. A moment too late to disguise her interest, she dragged her eyes up to meet his, flushing to her hairline. He was in time to squelch his smirk, which—he was certain—would not find favour with her.

"My aunt sent me to let you know there is warm water in the scullery, for you to refresh yourself," she said, her gaze now fixed on the rafters of the shed and her voice higher pitched than usual.

"Thank you." Philip reached for his shirt, then changed his mind and bundled it in his jacket, pulling on his great coat instead. He'd been perspiring freely while chopping, and would like to wash before dressing again, but even in the shelter of the shed he could feel the chill now he'd stopped.

The rain had cleared for now, and the afternoon was fair but cold, with a biting wind that hissed across the small kitchen courtyard and infiltrated beneath the skirts of his coat.

Lalamani was halfway to the house before he caught up with her. "I have a stack of wood we've cleared from the buildings at the Hall, Miss Finchurch. I'll have a cart load chopped into manageable pieces and send it over."

"That would be very kind of you," she said.

He cleaned himself as best he could in the scullery, grateful for the warm water and a handful of soap jelly. Beyond the door to the kitchen, he heard her telling Mrs Thorpe of his offer. He dried himself off and dressed again, resigned to being thanked, and sure enough, though he assured Mrs Thorpe the scraps he planned to give her were destined to burn and might as well provide someone with warmth while doing so, he had to bear the burden of her gratitude until the first of the afternoon callers arrived.

He had intended to leave in proper form after the civil thirty minutes. But Arthur Picknell annoyed him, with his sullen and reluctant attentions to Lalamani, and the other puppies accompanying their mothers were no better. And so Philip appropriated for himself the duties and privileges of a nephew of the house, even to addressing Mrs Thorpe as Aunt Hannah, and advising one over-enthusiastic youth to mind his manners.

Aunt Hannah failed to notice. Lalamani's glare promised retribution, but she went along with his masquerade until the last of the afternoon visitors was escorted to the door, and even then, allowed him to make his own farewells and escape into the evening.

LORD CALNE'S CHRISTMAS RUBY

Chapter Seven

It was a reprieve only, and when he stopped work the following day to let the men go home for their nooning and saw Lalamani waiting for him, he knew he would need to account for his sudden desire to slay dragons for her, or—failing a good fire breather—to protect her from nuisance. Though he doubted he could explain. He had spent the past evening and all day so far today trying to understand it himself.

"I am sent with food, Lord Calne," his damsel told him. "Our Aunt Hannah is anxious her new nephew should not starve."

"About that." He trailed her to where she had set a blanket in a patch of weak sunlight against the one stone wall still standing from the carriage house. "I can explain."

"What did you think you were doing?" She sounded more bemused than annoyed. "If you sought to convince those silly women and their sons you are courting me, I cannot fathom the purpose. And it won't serve, since you will be gone soon. Besides. It is ridiculous."

He had been intending to apologise, but that distracted him. "How is it ridiculous? That a poverty-stricken engineer like me might look so far above him?"

"That is not what I mean, and you know it. You are an earl, even if none of them realise it. And only an idiot would mistake you for anything but a gentleman. While I am daughter and niece to a merchant, without a drop of blue blood in my veins. Which at least means no one will be surprised when you disappear. They will simply decide you could not stomach the smell of the shop."

That sounded like a quote. From those women he'd interrupted at the Haverfords' dance, no doubt, or others just like them. Philip swallowed the urge to tell her what he really thought of her. For one thing, she wouldn't believe him. For another, he couldn't act on his feelings. Yes, she had more than enough money for both of them, but if he found the idea of marrying an heiress undesirable in the abstract, he discovered it was even more distasteful now he had found an heiress he could fall in love with. He could never consent to touching the money her uncle left her. And without it, he could not afford to marry.

"I do have to leave," he said. "But I am torn to pieces about it. For one thing, working here brings back all my father's stories. He grew up here, and used often to tell us stories about him and his younger brother, and the games they played in the grounds and in the dower house where they lived. I thought it would be no hardship to sell a place I had never seen, and didn't want to inherit. But it is wound around my bones, thanks to my father."

Lalamani's eyes widened. "You plan to sell? But what of the entail?"

"There is none. An entail must be renewed from time to time, and my cousin outlived my uncle long enough to inherit. The earl had sold everything that was his to sell, even the lands around here he acquired through enclosure, but under the entail he held the Hall in trust for his son, and his son held it in trust for the next heir."

"You."

It was not a question, but he confirmed it anyway. "Me. Because my cousin didn't renew the entail, I inherited free and clear. Apart from mountainous debts, which I have no way of paying except for selling what is left." Whether he wanted to or not.

Lalamani passed him a cup of something from a flask, and he took a sip. A lemon drink, still warm and rich with honey.

"You said that was one of the reasons you feel torn."

"I feel guilty about leaving the local people to the non-existent mercies of the local gentry. I have heard a few stories this week, and they're suffering. You'd think the rector would champion them, but... Well. You heard him yesterday. And according to those I've spoken with, he was the power behind the enclosure act, and is ruthless in collecting his tithes."

"But what can you do about it," Lalamani asked.

"I am the earl. I hold his living. I could show by example how to act. If I could stay."

He was going to tell her his third reason, which was his attraction to her, but he suddenly realised that, in connection to the first two, it would sound as if he was trying to persuade her to put her fortune at his disposal. And it was the rest of her assets he wanted. Her charm, her intelligence, her sense of humour, her delectable body.

"Come on," he said, scrambling to his feet. "Let me show you around and tell you what I'm doing."

He found himself sharing the stories he'd had from his father, who had known every inch of these lands where he and his twin had roamed until Gerard died and Hugo was sent to school, seldom to return.

Lalamani took Lord Carne a midday meal the next day, too. And the day after.

When she slipped up and called him 'my lord' in front of the workmen, he brushed it off with a laugh, but after they had left, asked her to call him Philip. "For if I have adopted Mrs Thorpe as my aunt, you must be my cousin," he suggested.

"Or your sister?"

He froze, every muscle alert, his eyes suddenly intent. "Definitely not my sister."

She couldn't look away. The conversation of the departing workmen faded and the corner they had chosen as their own picnic spot dimmed. Philip was suddenly more real than all of it; the only solid thing in a ghostly world. She swayed towards him and he gripped her shoulders, his eyes fixed on her lips, his face moving towards her… Until he straightened and turned away.

"I beg your pardon, Miss Finchurch." He kept his back to her, as if the ruin of his Hall was far more appealing than one slightly over-aged spinster.

He must have heard her sigh, because he spun round to face her. "You must know that, if circumstances were different…"

Was she supposed to believe she had swept him off his feet and he was only resisting with difficulty? What he took from her expression she didn't know, but he suddenly swore, and reached again for her shoulders, crushed her to him, then cursed again and lifted her bodily onto the log they had been using for a seat.

Now her head was a little higher than his, so she had to curve her neck to reach his lips when he lifted his face. She had been kissed before, a few times. Some of the ambitious young men who thought to win her uncle's favour had been almost convincing in their courtship. Besides, she was as susceptible as anyone to curiosity and the temptation of a private spot in a warm lush garden after a night of music and dancing. On the whole, the experiences had been unremarkable.

She could, were she not so distracted by his firm but gentle lips, catalogue the many differences between those disappointing kisses of long ago and this one, from the setting to the sensations. But he was running his tongue gently along her lips, and she opened, wondering what he intended, then forgetting everything. The oak, the chill wind, the possibility a workman might return early. Philip was all that existed in the world. Philip, and her body coming alive where he touched her, still only with his lips, and a hand lightly kneading each hip.

Until he groaned and wrapped his arms around her, pulling her from the log to mould her against him, his mouth hardening over hers, his tongue stroking even deeper over hers as she clasped him back and lifted her legs to curve them around his hips, heedless of anything except the urge to be closer still.

For one long endless moment, she was lost in sensation, and then he drew his head back, to drop a flurry of kisses along her jaw bone, so she tipped her head back to give him access, and blinked as a large rain drop fell in her eye.

It was followed by others, first a spattering, then a deluge, and Philip stumbled a couple of steps to set her down against the trunk, out of the rain.

His laugh was rueful, and his voice shook as he said, "They said in the inn last night that the rain would set in this afternoon."

He still held her, and she leant against him, uncertain her legs would hold her up. "That was…" She didn't have the words. "Philip," she said, instead. A statement, because she was afraid to make it a question.

"Lalamani," he breathed back, and rested his chin on her head, which had somehow lost its bonnet in the past fifteen minutes. One hand rested on her waist while the other stroked her back. "Lalamani," he said again, then, just as quietly, murmuring into her hair. "I owe you an apology, but I am not sorry. To have missed that kiss would have been a crime. But I had no right."

His obtuse male attitude steadied her, and her own voice was calm as she reminded him, "If any apology is required, it is for me to offer it. I started our kiss. And I am not sorry, either."

He chuckled. "I am glad. But I still... Were circumstances different, I could court you in proper form and hope one day for the privilege of taking our kiss to its proper conclusion, but I have nothing to offer a wife, Lalamani. It could be five years before the canal pays enough to provide more than bachelor accommodations. Even were you not used to the best of everything, I could not..." He trailed off.

"I do not need someone to provide for me," Lalamani reminded him. "I have more than enough money for me and anyone I truly loved." That was as close to a declaration as she dared, but it did not have the desired effect.

"Ah, Lalamani." He sighed, then kissed her again, a light touch on the forehead, and pulled away. "I cannot live off my wife. Can I?" He shook his head as if to clear it, then held out his undamaged hand. "Come. I should see you home to your aunt's house."

Ridiculous man. In their conversations, and in that kiss, she had glimpsed a hope for which she had thought herself too old. If he didn't see it too, or if he would let his male pride stand in its way, then she was too proud to pursue it. "I will show you a quicker way," she said. "There is a path and a gate straight to the house."

They ran through the rain hand in hand, and arrived at the house's side door, wet and laughing, the awkwardness left behind at the tumbledown Hall.

"Was this once part of the estate?" Philip asked, as he sat in the parlour rubbing his hair dry with a towel.

"It was the dower house," Aunt Hannah told him. "The earl sold it after his mother died, though by rights it should have gone to his youngest son. But, of course, young Hugo had been gone for many years by then."

"The dower house?" Philip was looking around, wide eyed.

Aunt Hannah lowered her voice so it did not carry beyond the room. "Yes, my lord. This was the home of your great grandmother, for whom you are named. Your father and uncle grew up here."

Lalamani looked from her aunt to the earl. His eyes were round with shock. He pulled himself together enough to close his gaping mouth. "You knew?"

"I was rector's wife here for forty years, Lord Calne. I knew all the Daventrys, especially the Dowager Lady Calne, who raised your father and uncle after their mother died. I daresay you think if the villagers knew you were the earl they would expect you to solve all their problems overnight. I do not blame you for keeping your identity hidden until you work out how you can do your best for your people. Do not worry. I will keep your secret. And so will Addy, of course."

Milly came in just then carrying a tray of tea makings, and Aunt Hannah changed the subject.

"It is so delightful to have plenty of tea, dear Lalamani. I do enjoy it, though one should not be attached to worldly things."

Philip was reeling. His father had loved the house in which he and his twin had grown, exiled from the Hall when his mother died shortly after their birth. Loved it, at least, until the incident that had cost him his brother. It must have been before Mrs Thorpe arrived in the parish, but perhaps she could answer some of the questions Philip had always had about his father's family. Surely people had talked, and if they talked to anyone, it would have been to the rector or his wife.

And she took it for granted he planned to stay. He wished he could. Not just so he could court Lalamani, but so he could do his duty by the people who had served the earldom for many generations.

There was one possibility, and to follow it through he would have to disclose his identity. The villagers would not be impressed with his deception, but perhaps they'd be grateful at the unmasking of a villain.

When a break in the rain came, he said his farewells. "I will be sure to bring an umbrella next time I come," he said.

"Will you come to dinner this evening," Mrs Thorpe suggested. "We always have the rector and his sister on the third Thursday of the month, so you would have fine company."

Philip accepted. Meeting the rector on a social occasion would suit his purposes nicely.

Mrs Thorpe smiled. "Excellent. And Lalamani shall enjoy having a young person to talk to; for we have been deserted by our usual visitors, Lord Calne. Mr Daventry, I mean."

"Please call me 'Philip'," he suggested. "After all, you knew my father and my great grandmother, so I am practically family."

Mrs Thorpe's eyes twinkled. "If you call me 'Aunt Hannah'."

Lalamani scrambled to her feet. "I shall walk you to the Hall gates," she said.

Within minutes, she had fetched her pelisse and bonnet and they were strolling up the lane, dodging the worst of the puddles.

Lalamani tucked her hand confidingly into his elbow. "Philip, I cannot be sure, but I suspect the Reverend Wagley of wickedness. Will you help me find out?"

Philip nodded. He would do more than help. After all, this was his business, and he said so. "I intend to unmask him, Lalamani. If he has been stealing the earldom's rents, perhaps for years, then he has to be stopped. And if I can recover any of the moneys, they should go back into the estate. Perhaps there will be enough..."

But he trailed off. She had stopped and was staring at him in surprise. "He has been stealing the rents?"

"He has been collecting the rents, according to the tenants to whom I've spoken, and my lawyer denies ever seeing them. One of them is lying."

"The rector, certainly, for I am sure he has been stealing from Aunt Hannah. You will help me, will you not? You don't have to leave the village yet?"

If Lalamani was heading into danger, the whole of Napoleon's army wouldn't be able to shift him from her side.

"Tell me," he suggested, and when she told him the whole story, he agreed it sounded suspicious.

"Write to your uncle's man of business and ask him for the details of the inheritance and the trust," he advised. "I'll find out how to get the letter to the mail collection point." He corrected himself. "Your man of business, now, of course."

"I wish he thought so." Lalamani sighed. "In his mind, Mr Wiggens still works for Uncle Hadley. 'A young lady like yourself, Miss Finchurch, need not worry her pretty little head about figures and other such fusty stuff.' I look forward to the day I turn twenty-five and can find a man of business who does not think a woman incapable of thinking."

"Does he know you were your uncle's secretary and managed all of his affairs from the time you were seventeen?"

"He is convinced I wrote to my uncle's dictation. He disapproves. He tells me Uncle should have sent me home when I was seventeen 'so you could make your curtesy to the Queen, Miss Finchurch.' So I could catch a husband before I become so elderly, he means."

They had reached the gates to the Hall's coach road, and before they parted, Philip enjoined Lalamani not to let the rector know of her suspicions. "We do not want to give him time to cover his tracks," he said. "If he has been stealing from your aunt, we'd do better to surprise him with the evidence."

Lalamani turned back. Philip walked the rest of the way into the village, turning what he'd learned over in his mind.

Perhaps he should take Lalamani's letter up to London himself. Interviewing Mr Wiggens could be useful. But first he wanted to meet this villainous rector.

Chapter Eight

Lalamani joined Aunt Hannah and Addy in the kitchen to help cook dinner, overriding her aunt's objections.

Lalamani took the opportunity to try to persuade Aunt Hannah someone had been stealing from her. The suggestion fell on deaf ears. Aunt Hannah could not believe it. Certainly, it could not be Dr Wagley. The mind revolted! He might be a little strict, Aunt Hannah conceded, but no one could doubt his faith. His sermons were thirty minutes long! He always knew the right passage from Scripture to show others the errors of their ways. No, Dr Wagley was a fine Christian man, though not, perhaps, as generous to the poor as her own dear Mr Thorpe.

Perhaps Dr Wagley's way was better. He said helping the poor only made them lazy. But Aunt Hannah sounded doubtful. "My dear Mr Thorpe said all of us faced trouble in our lives, and the good Lord wanted us to help others when they were in need."

Lalamani carefully studied the gingerbread stars she was icing to decide whether she should add more lines. "I like that, Aunt Hannah. He sounds lovely."

"He was, dear. Such a kind man. It did cause trouble sometimes, because he hated upsetting people. I remember one Easter when he gave three different women the lead solo, and the time he wanted to add five more grand prizes at the Whitsunweek fete, because he didn't want any of the entrants to be disappointed. The people loved him, dear, and they were all very helpful when I explained."

Lalamani managed to keep her face and her voice neutral. "Dr Wagley does not experience the same difficulty, I take it."

"Oh no, dear. Dr Wagley is very decisive. Of course, we do not have the fete any more. Dr Wagley felt it was a pagan festival and promoted licentious and debauched behaviour. And we do not have women in the psalm singers anymore." Aunt Hannah sighed. "I am sure it is all for the best."

Addy, who had been returning the chicken to its pot after turning it, slammed the lid back onto the dutch oven with quite unnecessary force. "Handsome is as handsome does," she muttered.

"He is very good about visiting the sick, Addy," Aunt Hannah said, but Addy just snorted.

With the three of them working, an expansive if simple dinner was ready for Addy and Milly to put on the table when Philip and the Wagleys arrived.

From behind the curtain in the parlour, Lalamani saw Philip arrive at the gate just as the Wagley's gig pulled up. The two who descended, as Lalamani had noticed at church, were male and female counterparts: tall, gaunt, and elderly; spry, but a little bent. They put Lalamani in mind of herons—sharp features and an alert forward-leaning stance.

Lalamani flicked the curtain back into place and hurried into the front hall in time to introduce Philip.

"Allow me to present Philip Daventry, who works for the Earl of Calne."

Two pair of pale eyes fixed first on Lalamani and then on Philip. Brother and sister both, Lalamani noted, jutted their chins forward and lengthened their necks, increasing the resemblance to herons. Dr Wagley, dressed top to toe in black, relieved only by a white stock, clearly stinted nothing on the cut and quality of his cloth, and Miss Wagley's grey silk gown was trimmed with, if Lalamani was not mistaken, real French lace. The contrast between their finery and Aunt Hannah's worn and much-mended widow's wear could scarcely be greater.

Dr Wagley surveyed Philip from top to toe, and asked, coldly, "And what do you do here, sirrah? The people of this village think highly of Mrs Thorpe, and will not see her put upon."

"I'm glad to hear it, Dr Wagley," Philip answered mildly. "I am here to survey the Hall, to decide what repairs are necessary."

Miss Wagley furrowed her brow. "You are a Daventry? How closely related are you to the earl, Mr Daventry?"

"The late earl was a connection of my father's," Philip prevaricated.

"Did you hear that, Jeremiah?" Miss Wagley tugged on her brother's arm, but Wagley's harrumph suggested he was not impressed.

The conversation in the parlour limped from one pronouncement by Dr Wagley after another. He frowned upon the evangelical fervour gripping a nearby parish, was suspicious about the proposed Act of Union, despised the call by radicals to widen the vote, and was scathing about the Speenhamland system of poor relief.

Addy's invitation to the dining room interrupted a homily on the place of women—silent and obedient.

Over dinner, Lalamani made an effort to turn the conversation. "Mr Daventry was formerly in the army. Before you arrived, he was telling us a little about the markets in Egypt."

Dr Wagley looked dourer than before. "Nothing unsuitable for a lady, I trust."

"Oh, Jeremiah," his sister chirped, "Mr Daventry is a gentleman; a relative of Calne, you know."

Philip, catching Lalamani's desperate eye-roll, picked up the conversational ball with a story about a carpet he and his friends had bargained for and how language difficulties had almost left them with a camel instead. He made an amusing tale of it, but only Lalamani laughed.

Dr Wagley spoke into the pause. "Another excellent meal, Mrs Thorpe. Mrs Thorpe sets a fine table, Daventry."

Lalamani did not try to resist the impulse. "My aunt is very grateful for the charity of the people of the parish, Dr Wagley, without which she would undoubtedly starve. Though…"

She felt a blow on her ankle. Philip, who had clearly guessed she was about to mention her uncle's provision for his sister. She shot him an accusing glance, but pressed her lips tightly together.

"The care of widows," Dr Wagley opined, "is, of course, enjoined on us in Scripture. 'But if any provide not for his own, and especially for those of his own house, he hath denied the faith, and is worse than an infidel.' Charity begins at home." He nodded seriously and took another mouthful of the donated chicken.

"And," his sister added, "it is the duty of every Christian to support the men of the cloth." She poked suspiciously at the chicken. "I would not like to think our parishioners were stinting their duty."

"Now, now, Euphrania," Dr Wagley said. "We do not begrudge Mrs Thorpe a chicken or two, especially when she has visitors. Do you make a long stay, Miss Finchurch? It would not do for you to be a charge on your aunt." He cast her an admonishing stare over the top of his glasses, which had slipped almost to the tip of his nose.

"My plans are not fixed, Dr Wagley." Lalamani was going to ask how it was his affair, but Philip spoke first, once again preventing her from antagonising the sour old man.

"How nice that you are able to support your brother in his parish work, Miss Wagley."

Miss Wagley needed no encouragement to dominate the conversation for the rest of that remove and all of the next. According to her, the parish had been neglected before the Wagleys arrived, and the people sunk in idleness and dissolute living. She seemed completely oblivious to any distress she might be causing Aunt Hannah, and—indeed—Aunt Hannah seemed barely to be listening.

Dr Wagley, when his sister asked his opinion— which was often—declared his agreement, often backing it up with a biblical verse, mostly, Lalamani noted, from the old Testament.

For the rest, he applied himself to his dinner, trying all the dishes on the table, and eating his way through every serving. He only took over the discussion once, when Lalamani pointed out Christmas was less than two weeks away.

"Christmas? Christmas? We do not celebrate that pagan festival in this parish, Miss Finchurch." The rhetorical bit within his teeth, he declaimed for several minutes on the pagan origins of traditional Christmas activities and the likely eternal destination of those who succumbed to the lure of evergreen decorations and other more licentious activities he would scorn to describe in the hearing of a lady. He graced his sister with a bow of his head.

By the time he pushed back a little from the table, the other four had long finished. Aunt Hannah had been looking uncertainly from him to Lalamani for some time, clearly wondering if she should signal the ladies' departure from the table. Before she could make up her mind, though, Miss Wagley stood.

"Ladies," she announced, and led the way to the parlour next door.

The men didn't stay at the table above ten minutes, and shortly after they joined the ladies, the Wagleys' gig arrived, and they said their farewells.

Lalamani waited for them to offer Philip a lift back to the inn, which they would pass on the way to the rectory. He was moving his arm cautiously after all his work at the Hall, and would surely be better to ride rather than walk. The Wagleys, though, collected their coats and shawls, and moved towards the front door without any such offer.

"Dr Wagley," Lalamani said. "Would you have room in your gig for Mr Daventry? I believe his arm is paining him."

Philip's glare suggested a total lack of appropriate gratitude, but he recovered himself to thank Dr Wagley politely, and the three left together.

Much though Philip wanted to stay behind for another word with Lalamani, he was glad not to face that walk, especially since it was raining again. The ride was short, only a few minutes of Dr Wagley's chilly disapproval and Miss Wagley's clumsy sycophancy.

As he prepared for bed, he turned over what they'd found out in the course of the day. Dr Wagley was an unlikely villain, however disagreeable he might be. But unlikely was not impossible. Lalamani was adamant her man of business was honest: an income had been left and income there was none. And Uncle Henry swore by Philip's own man.

By the morning, he had a plan. He walked the distance to the house once more, this time through driving rain. Lalamani scolded him for coming out and set his coat to dripping in front of the kitchen fire.

He admired the voluminous apron protecting her day dress. It had been made for Aunt Hannah, clearly, and wrapped Lalamani's slender body completely.

"We are turning out the rest of the bed chambers," Lalamani explained.

"We need to talk, Lalamani." He broke off to greet the smiling Mrs Thorpe.

"So lovely to have company, Philip. Come and sit down. You find us at sixes and sevens, but we can find you a place to sit and a nice cup of tea."

"No, Aunt Hannah, I'm here to help. Many a time I've cleaned up after myself. Lead me to a broom or a dust cloth, and I'm your man."

"We'll talk when she has her rest," Lalamani murmured as she passed him a bucket and a rag.

They stopped for a bite to eat at noon, and then Aunt Hannah went off to her bed, "For I am not as young as I used to be, my dears," and Addy to her room off the kitchen.

"Milly, Mr Daventry and I have some paperwork to take care of." Lalamani sent her maid to doze by the kitchen fire.

In the parlour, Philip explained what he had in mind. He would write to Brigadier General Lord Henry Redepenning, his uncle, explain their concerns, and ask him to visit both men of business and investigate.

"And you're sure your uncle would not mind?"

"Not at all," Philip reassured her. His uncle would assume Philip's interest in the matter was personal and would do all he could for a potential Countess of Calne. And his uncle would not be wrong, if Philip could find a way to provide for a wife without depending on her own wealth.

Together, they composed a letter, with many starts, stops, and insertions.

"There," Philip said after a while. "I think we have it."

"Give it here, Philip, and I'll write it out again."

Philip went off to put the kettle on the fire for another pot of tea, and Lalamani took their much-crossed draft to write it in a fair hand.

Chapter Nine

The rain set in for several days. Each morning, Philip made the trek to the house, declaring he could do no work at the Hall until the weather cleared. Aunt Hannah cheerfully accepted his presence without any comment beyond declaring they would eat their main meal in the middle of the day, "as the country people do, Philip," so he had only the one trip each day, and would not be walking in the rain and the dark.

Lalamani didn't comment either. She held herself at a slight distance, and Philip—conscious of his new feelings for her, but unclear about how she felt—did not try to bridge the gap. These days of domesticity were peaceful and pleasant.

Philip joined Lalamani in the kitchen, where she made gingerbread shapes and other Christmas treats, and he brought a huge box of ribbons down from the attic so she could concoct Christmas decorations to put up on Christmas Eve. He helped clean, mend, and even paint until the whole house was gleaming.

One day he ventured down into the cellars, which had loomed in his childhood as the gateway to hell. His father had spoken briefly of that watershed moment in his own childhood. Philip told Lalamani the story, holding her hand against the chill that had leaked into his soul from his father's memories.

Hugo Daventry's older brother, Walter, had locked Hugo and Gerard in their grandmother's cellar, then gone home and told no one they were there. Perhaps the older boy had not known Lady Calne was assisting at a birth and the servants were on their Sunday half-day. Or perhaps he intended the twins not to be found for twelve hours. Both boys had been chilled, and Gerard, already sick with a winter ague, had never recovered, dying several days later.

"My grandfather blamed my father," Philip told Lalamani. "His heir told him it was my father's idea, and my uncle tried to dissuade them. The earl believed Walter."

It was the beginning of the split in the family that became permanent when Hugo married a commoner, the younger sister of Lord Henry Redepenning's wife.

The cellar lost its terror after he told Lalamani its history, and it desperately needed sorting, so he spent an afternoon down there putting items on shelves and hauling the obvious rubbish outside for disposal.

One room on the lower side of the house, with a row of high windows letting in the light, had obviously been a play place for the twins, and perhaps previous generations of grandchildren, for Philip found the detritus of their games, and smiled as he recognised signifiers of some of his father's stories: a chest full of glass and gilt jewellery and costume crowns that had featured as a pirate's treasure, a pair of wooden swords and lozenge shaped shields on which the painted crosses still shone after he wiped off the dirt, a box filled with a carved army—no, two armies—their colours still discernible, though chipped and scratched after years of playing. Philip put those treasures on a shelf. He'd ask Aunt Hannah, later, if he might have them.

In the evenings, he mixed with the local patrons of the inn and found the village sharply divided in their opinions. Miss Wagley was roundly condemned by one and all as an interfering old besom, but Dr Wagley was regarded as a saint in some quarters and a tyrant in others. As the chairman of the workhouse committee and wielder of influence with the squire and therefore the constable, even those who didn't like him feared to cross him.

On the evening of the fifth day, Philip arrived back at the inn just as a travelling coach pulled in. He'd passed it and was climbing the stairs when a familiar voice said, "Good day, my boy."

Brigadier General Lord Henry Redepenning had just entered the main doors, a small, thin bespectacled man at his shoulder.

Philip turned, retracing his steps with his hand extended. "Uncle! What on earth are you doing here?"

"It's good to see you, too, Philip." His uncle grinned.

"I'm delighted, of course. I just didn't expect you to post all the way out here."

"Thought I'd bring Wiggens." He waved to his travelling companion. "Wiggens, my nephew."

The little man was clutching a briefcase with one hand and a file folder with the other. He managed to bow with a degree of dignity. "A bad business, my l—Mr Daventry. A bad business."

"Which we will not discuss in the public entrance of the inn," Uncle Henry said. "What are the rooms like here, my boy?"

Philip escorted them in, saw them settled with rooms, and ordered a nice dinner to be served in a private parlour, where he met with his uncle a short while later.

Mr Wiggens was anxious to talk to Dr Wagley that very evening, but Philip insisted they wait to consult with Mrs Thorpe and her niece, and Uncle Henry supported him.

Over a dinner served by Uncle Henry's own manservant, Philip questioned the two older men. Beyond a doubt, the rector had been sent funds intended for Aunt Hannah. And Uncle Henry also confirmed Philip's estate had received no rentals since the steward disappeared five years ago. "It is a substantial sum, my boy," Uncle Henry said. "Let's hope we can recover some."

The following morning, Philip escorted his uncle and the man of business on the two-mile walk to Aunt Hannah's. Uncle Henry, country born and still a fit active man in his early sixties, thoroughly enjoyed the trek. The rain had cleared, and the mud had dried between the ruts so that, by stepping carefully, one could avoid the worst of the puddles.

Mr Wiggens regarded the hedgerows with suspicion, the sheep with distaste, and the cows with alarm.

"You are not accustomed to the country, Mr Wiggens," Philip observed.

"I am a London man, sir. This place… the noises, the smells, the animals… How do people stand it?"

"Country people say the same when they come to London," Uncle Henry said. "But you were here once before, Wiggens?"

"Yes, my lord, when I came down to—as I thought—put in place measures for Mrs Thorpe's welfare. I blame myself, my lord. I blame myself very much. Had I not been so anxious to return to London… But a gentleman of the cloth, my lord, and so concerned for her, seemingly!"

"Yes, well, what's done is done, Wiggens. Is this the place, Philip? But I have been here before! Visiting your great grandmother with your father, Philip. It is surely the estate's dower house."

In the thin winter sunshine, it looked better than it had on Philip's first visit. The windows sparkled, cleaned inside and out, Lalamani had holystoned the front door slab and Philip had painted the front door a fresh green.

Philip had sent the pot boy ahead of them to warn the ladies of the visit, and morning tea was laid out in the parlour, where Aunt Hannah waited to preside over the tea pot, still in her faded black, but with a clean white fichu Lalamani had brought for her and a white lace cap decorated with pretty pink ribbons Philip had watched Lalamani making one afternoon while Mrs Thorpe slept.

"Lord Henry, this is such an honour. I do not know if you remember me, my lord, but I had the privilege of meeting you when you came here with the earl's father. Back when you were at school, that would have been."

"Indeed I remember," Uncle Henry agreed, bowing over her hand. "You gave us a great slab of gingerbread each. I still remember how delicious it was."

Aunt Hannah beamed. "Won't you take a seat, my lord? And, Mr Wiggens, how very kind of you to come all this way. Please sit down, sir. How very delightful this is, to be sure. Why, I do not remember when I last had such visitors."

Philip waited for her to get over her first fluster and to pour tea for Lalamani to carry to each of the guests. Once everyone was settled, he turned to Mr Wiggens. "Mr Wiggens, will you explain to Mrs Thorpe why we are here today?"

"Oh dear," Mr Wiggens said. He put down his cup, pulled some papers out of his omnipresent briefcase, and pushed his glasses back up his nose. "Mrs Thorpe, may I first say how very, very sorry I am."

Aunt Hannah was bewildered. "Why, whatever can you mean, Mr Wiggens?"

Slowly, the story came out, with many interruptions and exclamations from Aunt Hannah. Wiggens had come to the village to make sure his client's sister had a house to live in and an income to keep her comfortable for the rest of her life, as instructed by his client. "Your brother's instructions were very clear, Mrs Thorpe."

He'd found the village in some disarray even months after the epidemic that had carried off many, though mostly the elderly and the very young. The new rector had been in place a mere few weeks, and was working heroically. He much impressed Mr Wiggens with his commitment to returning order to the parish. Mrs Thorpe was sick, and—while past the crisis—in no fit state to hear business arrangements.

This, Mr Wiggens had from Dr Wagley and his sister, who assured Mr Wiggens that Mrs Thorpe had asked the Wagleys to take care of the matter for her.

"I never did! Oh, I never did." Aunt Hannah held out her hand, and Lalamani clasped it. "Lalamani, dear, how could they have said such a thing?"

Mr Wiggens, anxious to escape the uncertain countryside for the safety of his beloved London, had accepted Dr Wagley's offer to manage everything for Mrs Thorpe: the purchase of a house and the payment of a quarterly income sufficient to keep the admiral's sister in comfort and to assure her of some of life's elegancies. Here, Mr Wiggens cast a scornful glance around the room.

He had insisted on seeing Mrs Thorpe's signature giving Dr Wagley power to act as her agent in all things. "This, ma'am, is the document Dr Wagley brought me. See, witnessed by Miss Wagley, and signed by you."

Aunt Hannah shook her head. "No, Mr Wiggens. No, I did not sign that document. Why, that does not even look like my signature." The ready tears were rolling down her cheeks again.

Lalamani perched on the arm of her aunt's chair, all the better to hold the poor lady and pat her comfortingly.

"Oh, Lalamani, I cannot bear to believe it," she wailed. After a few moments, she lifted her head and straightened her back. "I need to know, Mr Wiggens. Have you been paying money to Dr Wagley?"

"I have, ma'am. I have paid him the sum of three thousand four hundred pounds, at the rate of one hundred pounds per quarter. This does not include the money disbursed for the repairs and furnishing of this house." Again, Mr Wiggens frowned at the shabby sofa and chairs. "A further sum, ma'am, of one hundred and seventy-two pounds when the house was first purchased, and sixty-five pounds three years ago."

Aunt Hannah's mouth opened and shut a few times as she clearly considered and rejected several words. Philip was a bit taken aback himself. Clearly, very little of the money had made its way to its rightful owner.

Finally, Aunt Hannah spoke. "Why, that fiend. He has not given me a tenth of that, Mr Wiggens, Lord Henry, and every penny has come with a sermon about how one should not be extravagant when living on the generosity of others. Why, Lalamani, he made me feel so guilty, and so grateful, and all the time it was my money."

The tears were gone. The colour high in her cheeks, Aunt Hannah was fast working herself into a temper. "Why the evil, evil, lying thief. Evil to them who evil thinks, Lalamani, and so I trusted him and look what he had done. Stealing from me! When I think of all the people I could have helped. Why, Mrs Bascombe's baby might be alive this very day had I money for the doctor, and I begged Dr Wagley, but he just shook his head and said how sad it was."

She could sit no longer, but was marching up and down the little parlour, her skirts swishing as she flicked them round at each end of the room. "As for that sister of his. Oh, if he is in it, she is too, you can be sure. 'I would like to wear colours again,' I said to her. 'Do you forget your husband so easily?' said she. 'Those of us who were not blessed with the holy state of matrimony find that hard to understand. Many a widow would be grateful to have such good cloth to their back and many years of wear in it yet.' All the time, it is my money that puts the clothes on her back, and so I'll be bound."

She came to a stop in front of Lord Henry. "You will put a stop to it, Lord Henry, will you not? Why, I should like to… I do not know what, indeed I do not, but it would be violent, beyond a doubt."

Philip met Lalamani's eyes, brimming with amusement at the sight of her plump little hen of an aunt ready for war. "This is the most animated I've seen her," he murmured.

"Just think," she whispered back, "I will never again have to listen to 'But Dr Wagley says…'"

Lord Henry broke away from the conversation he and Mr Wiggens were having with Aunt Hannah to say, "Philip, we will head to the rectory immediately to confront the gentleman. You will come?"

"Of course, sir," Philip agreed readily.

"I will not come," Aunt Hannah said, decidedly, "for I would not be responsible for my actions, Lord Henry. But, Lalamani, you shall go in my stead. I trust you to remain calm, my dear, and to come back and tell me all about it. Now send in Addy, so I might tell her. Why, my dear, next quarter day, I will be able to pay Addy her wages and buy her a new dress! Just think!"

"I am authorised to pay you a sum immediately, ma'am," Mr Wiggens assured her. "Even if my firm cannot recover the amount already disbursed, we cannot but feel responsible for your loss. I am authorised to pay you two hundred pounds pending further investigations."

Lalamani left Addy ensconced in the other comfortable chair by the fire, holding her mistress's hands, the two excitedly planning what they would do with the unbelievable wealth of two hundred pounds while Milly prepared them a fresh pot of tea.

Bless them. They had already, in their minds, outfitted the children of several local families with shoes against the cold and had cut back their own plans for a whole new wardrobe to accommodate a new dress for the eldest daughter of the Mrs

Bascombe mentioned earlier. "For she has grown so much this last season, her skirts are up to her knees, and she cannot easily pin her bodice closed.

"I fear the boys have noticed already, and it may be a matter of shutting the stable door after the horse has bolted, but there's no use that villain preaching from the altar about girls being improperly dressed when the family does not have any way of buying cloth for a new dress. Oh, it makes me so wild, Addy, when I think of it. Why the she-fiend could have long since given the child one of the dresses that *I paid for*."

Lalamani closed the door on the rest of the conversation and joined the three men where they waited for her in the porch.

At the rectory, they surprised Dr Wagley crossing from the house to the church. He stopped to let them catch up, his eyes wary behind his spectacles.

"Dr Wagley? I am Brigadier General Lord Henry Redepenning. Mr Wiggens I think you know. And, of course, my nephew and Miss Finchurch. We wish to have a word with you."

Dr Wagley started walking again, saying over his shoulder, "It will have to wait, sir. I am on my way to God's house for my daily devotions."

Philip moved to block him, while Lord Henry stopped him with, "Halt!" After that parade-ground bark, the Brigadier General dropped his voice to a low growl. "You, Dr Wagley, have some explanations to make, and we will hear them now."

Dr Wagley, his gaze darting from person to person, hesitated on the path. Suddenly, he rounded on Lalamani. "What are you doing here? You're not part of this. You shouldn't be here."

Lalamani took a step back in alarm. The man was almost foaming at the mouth, his pale eyes protruding from his head in the force of his anger.

Philip stepped beside her, placing his shoulder before her as if he feared a physical attack. Indeed, the rector seemed ready to explode, until Lord Henry said sharply, "That will be quite enough, sirrah. Miss Finchurch is here to represent her uncle's wishes and her aunt's interests."

Dr Wagley turned his wrathful eyes on the older man. "She is a woman, sir. She should be silent and obedient. At her age, she should be married and have several children, not traipsing all over the countryside with an…" he nearly spat the next word, "engineer."

"Enough!" Lord Henry's battle-field roar silenced the fulminating rector mid-rant.

With several resentful glances at Lalamani, and defiantly proud glares at the men, he led the way to his study. He denied nothing, but insisted he was on the Lord's work and was therefore above mere human rules. "Mrs Thorpe would only have frittered the money away. What was her brother thinking, leaving such a legacy to a woman? Ridiculous. I have made much better use of it. Why, I reroofed the church. I put up a new wall to stop cows grazing in the church yard. I paid for building the extension to the workhouse."

"Correction," Lord Henry said, in a deceptively mild tone. "Mrs Thorpe paid for those things. And you gave her no choice in the matter."

Lalamani, who had been examining the rich furnishings in the rector's study, asked, "How much of Mrs Thorpe's income did you spend on furnishing the rectory, Dr Wagley? And on clothing for you and Miss Wagley?"

The rector glared at her, but made no reply.

"Mr Wiggens will examine your financial records," Lord Henry declared.

"He will also be looking for the rents collected from Lord Calne's tenants," Philip added.

"Those rents are nothing to do with you," Wagley hissed. "I collected them on behalf of the Earl of Calne."

"Yet the earl's man of business has no record of their receipt," Lord Henry said. "I examined the books myself."

"How dare you!" Wagley was dancing in his rage. "You are interfering without right or justice. I shall complain to the Bishop. I shall complain to the earl."

Philip, who had remained seating while the rector stood to better express his fury, was forming a peak with the fingers of both hands, his gaze intent on pushing his deformed fingers into place. "I asked my uncle to investigate, and he did so on my authority." He shot a piercing glance at Wagley over his steepled hands. "As is my right and duty, as Earl of Calne."

Wagley froze, then broke into a frenzied diatribe about deceit and his duty to rescue the earldom's funds from a profligate who would only waste them on riotous living.

Eventually, Lord Henry shouted him into silence, and Wagley sullenly produced a tidy set of ledgers in which every expenditure had been meticulously recorded. "Scripture says, 'Thou shalt not muzzle the ox that treadeth the corn,'" he declared, "and again, 'A workman is worthy of his hire.'"

Despite his quotations of Scripture, the records in his own handwriting were damning, every receipt and expenditure meticulously detailed. Even the sceptical squire, sent for to officiate in his role as local magistrate, could not deny the evidence. Wagley and his sister were taken into custody, pending further examination.

Aunt Hannah was pleased to know the rector had salted away much of what he had stolen from her in savings and investments. It would take time, but Mr Wiggens thought he should be able to recover at least half of the purloined funds. "Your rentals, too, my lord," he assured Philip.

Chapter Ten

The Wagley's larceny was the wonder of the village, but it was overshadowed by the discovery that Mr Philip Daventry, the quiet-spoken engineer with the ready smile, was really the new Earl of Calne.

Lalamani informed Philip that the poorer villagers were happy to overlook the deception. Aunt Hannah's supporters deduced he had disguised himself at the service of catching out "that there Dr Wagley and his sister, and a good thing, too." Lord Calne was their hero, not least once the rectory maid spread the news his tenants' rentals had been stolen by the unloved pair.

She left unexpressed their expectation that Lord Calne would now stay and resolve all their ills, but Philip could read between the lines.

And he could. With the rents he would start to receive next quarter day, even if he reduced them to a level more in keeping with his tenant's ability to pay, and with the money from the earldom's other properties he had already ordered sold, he would be able to arrange part payments to the hovering creditors with the promise of the rest in quarterly payments over time. Better yet, Wagley's accounting book recorded investments and savings, some of which should come back to Philip once the courts had finished their slow work.

Meanwhile, the weight of villagers' hopes was in every look he received in the lanes, every curtsy or bow, or hand offered for him to shake.

The gentry, particularly those who had ignored the lowly engineer, were more inclined to take offence at his impersonation. Even those fathers and brothers of would-be countesses, sent to the inn to make Lord Calne's acquaintance, usually managed to work in an assurance they alone, of all the locals, would have kept Lord Calne's secret and assisted him in unmasking the villain.

The day after the confrontation, he and Lord Henry saw the Wagleys off to Horsham to await the assizes, escorted by a brace of constables, and Mr Wiggens onto the mail coach that would return him to the safety of London.

Lord Henry would leave the next day, going directly to his nephew's house in West Gloucestershire, where his family was gathering for Christmas. "You are welcome to join us, Philip, of course," he offered, as they strolled back to the inn after an afternoon visit to Aunt Hannah's house, "but I will not press you if you prefer to spend Christmas with your lady."

"Not mine, uncle, more's the pity. Even if we can recover some of the stolen rent money, I'll be in no position to take a wife for a long time, perhaps years. Especially if I choose to keep this estate, which I suppose I must. How can I ask her to wait?"

"Why should you wait? Miss Finchurch is a considerable heiress, and can well afford any level of comfortable living she requires."

"That makes it worse. The first time we met, she told me she would not marry a fortune hunter under any circumstances."

Lord Henry stopped, and regarded Philip solemnly. "Are you a fortune hunter, then?"

"Of course not! I wish she were of modest means, or even without a penny. She might consider me then."

Lord Henry strolled on, his hands clasped behind his back, his attention seemingly on the hedgerow on his side of the lane. "So, is it her pride that stands in the way of your marriage, or yours?"

It was Philip's turn to stop. "Pride?"

His uncle kept walking, looking back over his shoulder. "Of course, pride. You love each other, as is plain for all the world to see. You are not after her fortune, any more than she is after your title, which she is not, if that thought crossed your mind."

Philip denied it with a hasty gesture. "Of course, she is not after my title. If anything, she regards it as a hindrance."

"Just as you do her fortune. Think about it, Philip. You are both young, healthy, single, and in love. Between you, you have the means and social position to do and be whatever you want, as a couple and as a family. What can be keeping you apart, if not pride?" He carried on down the lane, clearly having said all he meant to say, for he turned the subject to the grandchildren who would be waiting to see him when he arrived for Christmas.

Philip was not required to do more than listen, which was just as well, for his mind was elsewhere, occupied in taking apart his set plans for his future and shuffling them into a more pleasing pattern. Uncle Henry was right. Or, at least, he was right about Philip. Lalamani was worth humbling himself for, and if he could not be as certain of her response as Uncle Henry seemed, he would at least put it to the test.

He would have returned to the house that very night, but he and Uncle Henry were promised to dinner at the squire's. Tomorrow would be soon enough, even if every minute between now and when he saw Lalamani again would be a lifetime.

Philip did not have, had never had, a valet. Except for his one excursion into London Society with his uncle, Philip happily dressed himself without assistance. He had done so, he told those who felt the dignity of an earl required a manservant, since he first went to school, and intended to do so ever more. But fashionable ball attire required a helper. And so, Philip found, did courting wear.

As they had on the night of the ball, Uncle Henry and his manservant hovered, advised, corrected, and occasionally took a direct hand in fitting him into his finest shirt, an intricately tied cravat, his best pair of moleskin pantaloons in a soft faun he could never wear on a building site, and an embroidered waistcoat he had regretted buying at the moment of purchase since he would never have a day occasion formal enough to require it. But today he was glad of it.

Next came boots polished to the highest shine they'd had since he brought them home from the bootmaker, and the jacket his friends had talked him into the day he bought the waistcoat. It took Uncle Henry and the manservant, working together, to coax his shoulders into the jacket.

The two of them exchanged a whisper, and the manservant left the room, to return a few minutes later with Uncle Henry's trinket box. Despite his protests, Philip found himself fitted with a gold cravat pin set with a small emerald and three dangling belt fobs.

Uncle Henry handed him his beaver top hat, and put on his own. Philip stood a moment more at the mirror, hoping he looked calmer than he felt. Turning to the door where the manservant waited with his great coat, he felt a momentary pang that it was such a workaday garment, which was silly, since he'd be removing it as soon as he arrived. Still, what would it have hurt to have allowed the tailor to add the extra capes he had suggested?

Uncle Henry's coach was already loaded; the horses harnessed and waiting. They were dropping Philip at the house on the way out of town, both Uncle Henry and his servant having forbidden Philip to walk in his finery. In moments, the trinket box had been restowed, and they were on their way.

For the few minutes of the trip, Philip kept his mind off the coming interview by sending messages to his cousins, but as the coach pulled up at the gate, Uncle Henry reached out to clasp his hand. "I will not get down, my boy, but will be on my way. You know I wish you every success. I like your young lady very much, and I am confident your father and mother would have approved. Write me a letter and tell me what she says, and I will expect an invitation to the wedding."

Lalamani was dusting the window ledge in the front room, watching the road because she hoped Philip would call in before he went to the work site. She stilled the duster as Lord Henry's coach pull up outside. After a moment, Philip descended. A transformed Philip, dressed as finely as a town buck. Where could he be going?

In here? Really? He opened the gate, and his face, looking up at the house, was anxious. Behind him, the carriage continued down the lane, so this must be his destination, all spruced up as if he was going courting.

At the thought, she dropped the duster and flew into the hall. "Milly," she called. "I need you."

How could he arrive in all his splendour and her in an old gown with a handkerchief to protect her hair and an apron tied around her twice because it was one of Aunt Hannah's.

Aunt Hannah and Addy had appeared at her call, as well as her own maid.

"Tell Lord Calne I will be down shortly," Lalamani instructed Addy, and hurried up the stairs, with Milly on her heels. "The rose morning gown.

No. What if he wants to take a walk? The light green, and put out the forest green pelisse and the matching bonnet. My hair! You must do something with my hair. Oh hurry, Milly."

What if he wasn't planning to propose? What if he had come to say goodbye, and Lord Henry was merely walking the horses until he had said his farewells? But the horses had been at a trot when they left, and in a direction that led out to the main road west.

What if he was all dressed up to visit one of the many gently-born maidens who had been trailed before him since he arrived? No. He had shown no signs of interest. But he wouldn't, would he? He was far too polite to make a show of courting one woman in from of another he had kissed.

While she fretted, Milly helped her out of her simple wool gown and into the fashionable silk, its vertical stripes alternating a soft green and a cream figured with embroidered sprigs of blossom in shades of lemon, with darker green leaves and stems.

How embarrassing if he guessed why she had changed. She almost told Milly to reverse the fastening she had just completed, and get her back into her working dress. But Milly was now brushing her hair, then combing it and pinning it into an elegant but simple twist at the back of her head. In the small mirror, she looked—not elegant, she was too short and curved for elegance—but at least armoured for an early call from the man who haunted her every waking thought.

A knock at the door heralded Aunt Hannah, broadly smiling. "Lalamani, you look lovely. Here. I would like you to wear this." She fumbled at her neck, undoing the cross that was one of the three pieces of jewellery she always wore. A locket with a picture of each of her brothers. A mourning brooch with locks of hair from her departed husband. And the cross Uncle Thorpe had given her as a wedding present.

"For luck, dearest." She dropped her voice. "He wants to see you alone. Oh, isn't it exciting? I could not be more pleased."

"Do you think he means to…" Lalamani let Milly fasten the chain around her neck, and stood to slip her feet into the slippers that matched the dress. "He said he could not court me; he could not live off his wife."

Aunt Hannah snorted. "What nonsense. Well, if he is not here to propose, I much mistake the matter. He loves you. That has been plain as the nose on my face since he first came running to the shop to see you before he had even washed away the dust of his journey."

Strengthened by her best morning dress, and Aunt Hannah's reassurance and warm hug, Lalamani made her way down the stairs, turning Aunt Hannah's parting advice over in her mind. "If he does not ask you to wed him, dear, you just ask him." She couldn't. Could she? Why not?

Philip was waiting in the parlour, standing by the mantelpiece looking into the fire. But he turned and straightened as she entered, and the devouring heat of his look made her suddenly shy, so that she retreated to formality. "Good morning, Lord Calne."

His smile faded. "Not Philip?"

Her own anxiety sank at the need to smooth the worried crease between his brows. "Of course, Philip. Let me start again. Hello, Philip. How nice to see you. I thought you would be at the Hall this morning."

"I have given my work crew a few days off. Until after St Stephen's Day. You look very lovely in that gown."

"You are rather smartly turned out yourself, today."

Philip looked down at himself, and chuckled. "I gave my uncle and his man their heads. You have guessed why, perhaps?"

Lalamani could feel herself blush, but Philip did not expect an answer, rushing on to say, "I prepared a speech. I spent the whole night rehearsing, I think. I may have slept a little, but only in snatches. And now I cannot remember a single word."

"I am sure it was excellent, but I do not need a speech," Lalamani told him.

He sank to one knee and took her hand. "I love you, Margaret Lalamani Finchurch. Would you do me the enormous honour of consenting to be my wife?"

It was speech enough, saying everything needed, and Lalamani's response needed only one word, but for a moment she could only stand looking down at his dear face, smiling. He beamed in return, but his smile slipped as the moment dragged on. "Lalamani?" he prompted.

"Yes. Oh yes, Philip. Oh Philip, I love you, too."

Chapter Eleven

Sunday was Christmas Eve. Philip was at the house early enough to escort his ladies to church, having once again hired the inn's gig. The curate from the next parish undoubtedly did an adequate job of the service, but Philip sailed through the morning in a dream, conscious of little but his betrothed.

He did notice the stir when he escorted Lalamani to take her rightful place beside him in the Calne box at the front of the church. Aunt Hannah, too, resplendent in the new gown Lalamani had made from the material they had been buying the day he came across them in the village shop.

Yes, and the even greater rustle and murmur when the curate read the banns for the first time.

After church, they ran the gauntlet of well-wishers, some sincerely delighted and others wanting the favour of their future countess. Philip hovered, but he need not have worried. Lalamani managed them with grace, and Aunt Hannah, who had known most of them since they were in swaddling, was at her elbow to support her.

A welcome flurry of rain, cold enough to hint at snow, sent everyone on their way. Yes, and would discourage afternoon visits, so he would have

Lalamani to himself, but for her aunt and the two maids.

Still, as they decorated the house that afternoon, he found plenty of opportunity for tender moments under the bunches of mistletoe he helped to hang, and less holiday-sanctioned kisses whenever he could get Lalamani alone and unobserved for a moment.

The shabby house quickly took on a Christmas gaiety, with evergreen swags and wreaths, kissing boughs, and hanging bunches of ribbons. Lalamani fetched some strings of glass beads to twine around the swags on the mantelpiece in the parlour, where they would sparkle in the candle-light.

"Pretty," Aunt Hannah declared. "Do you have any more?"

"Wait here," Philip commanded, and went to fetch his father's pirate chest from the cellar.

"Bring a sheet to put down on the parlour carpet," he suggested to Milly, as he passed her in the kitchen, and a few minutes later he deposited the chest in the middle of the sheet.

"These should clean up to be very pretty," he said. "Even the metal things." He rubbed a crown, and the metal under the dust gleamed in the trail of his finger. Aunt Hannah and Lalamani were silent, and he looked around to see them gaping at the chest.

"It cannot be. The Calne Treasure?" Aunt Hannah asked.

"A jackdaw's treasure most of it," Lalamani said, "but some of it..." She knelt beside him and pulled a necklace of red beads from the tangle, to rub them on her apron and hold them up to the light. "Philip, these are rubies. Very fine."

"Lady Calne's rubies!" Aunt Hannah touched them lightly, her face awed. "They went missing long before we came here to live. And all this time they have been in the cellar."

It took them the rest of the afternoon to pull everything out, cleaning them under Lalamani's direction and spreading them around the room. It was, as Lalamani said, the eclectic collection of a jackdaw, or an imaginative pair of boys, borrowing here and there, and interrupted before they could return what they'd taken. Some of the jewellery was genuine, and would bring a good price. A few items were antiquities in need of an expert appraisal. Most of the hoard was worthless, Lalamani said, but Philip disagreed. "Christmas decorations and children's toys have their own value," he said, draping a bright string of green glass beads across the mantlepiece.

Philip insisted the house belonged to Aunt Hannah, so the valuables were hers, but Aunt Hannah said it was the Calne Treasure, undoubtedly deposited in her cellar by his own father, so it was his. And, besides, she had everything she needed for the remainder of her life. And Lalamani and Philip were her only family, so they would just take the treasure and put it towards the cost of restoring the Hall, and say no more about it.

"So, Lord Calne," Lalamani said, when they had packed all the real treasures away except the ruby necklace and its matching earrings, which she had agreed to wear to the Christmas morning service, "you are now wealthy enough to give away rubies for Christmas when all I have for you is those embroidered slippers." She pointed to the comfortable knitted slippers she'd made with her own hands.

Philip heard the slight undercurrent of tension, and bent to kiss it out of her. "I have been a wealthy man since the day you looked on me with favour, Miss Finchurch. 'For your price is far above rubies.' You are my love, and with you by my side, all of this is trumpery. You, Lalamani Finchurch-soon-to-be-Daventry are my Christmas Ruby."

THE END

Jude Knight needs your help

Book reviews help readers to find books, and authors to find readers. Please consider writing a review for *Lord Calne's Christmas Ruby*, even a couple of sentences telling people what you liked (or didn't like) about it. Reviews can be posted on Goodreads and on most eretailers websites. For links to this book on those sites, see the *Lord Calne's Christmas Ruby* page on my website: http://judeknightauthor.com/books/lord-calnes-christmas-ruby/

News and special offers

Subscribe to Jude's newsletter for information about publication dates and more. As a subscriber, you will receive advance information about release dates and special price periods as well as exclusive, subscriber-only special offers. Jude sends a newsletter six times a year. New subscribers receive a link to a page full of free short stories and novellas to download as ebooks.

Subscribe to my newsletter

Acknowledgements

Thank you to my beta readers: Carol, Sue, Jocelyn, Tray-Ci, Sandy, Angie, Cathy, Elizabeth, and Doreen. Your comments and suggestions led to many changes that made the book stronger.

As always, a special thank you to my husband, without whose support I would probably forget to eat when I get stuck in the early nineteenth century, and to my sister Sue, who is always my first reader.

About the author

Jude Knight has always loved telling stories, mostly for the benefit of children in need of entertainment. Her strong determined heroines, heroes who appreciate them, and villains you'll love to loathe first made their way into the covers of a book three years ago. A dozen books later, the wind fills her sails and many more plots jostle for daylight.

Website and blog: http://judeknightauthor.com
Subscribe to newsletter: http://judeknightauthor.com/newsletter/
Facebook: https://www.facebook.com/JudeKnightAuthor/
Twitter: https://twitter.com/JudeKnightBooks
Pinterest: https://nz.pinterest.com/jknight1033/
Amazon author page: https://www.amazon.com/Jude-Knight/e/B00RG3SG7I

Regency books

Candle's Christmas Chair (A novella in *The Golden Redepennings* series)
They are separated by social standing and malicious lies. How can he convince her to give their love another chance?

Gingerbread Bride (A novella in *The Golden Redepenning* series)
Mary runs from an unwanted marriage and finds adventure, danger and her girlhood hero, coming once more to her rescue.

Farewell to Kindness (Book 1 in *The Golden Redepenning* series)
Love is not always convenient. Anne and Rede have different goals, but when their enemies join forces, so must they.

A Raging Madness (Book 2 in *The Golden Redepenning* series)
Their marriage is a fiction. Their enemies are all too real. The truth will need all the trust Ella and Alex can find.

A Baron for Becky
She was a fallen woman. How could the men who loved her help set her back on her feet?

Revealed in Mist
As spy and enquiry agent, Prue and David worked to uncover secrets, while hiding a few of their own.

A Suitable Husband
A chef from the slums, however talented, is no fit mate for the cousin of a duke, however distant. But Cedrica can dream.

Lunch-length reads: story collections

Hand-Turned Tales and *Lost in the Tale*
A double handful of short stories and novellas. Hand-Turned is free from most eretailers. Try the range of Jude's imagination one bite at a time, in a lunch-length read.

If Mistletoe Could Tell Tales
A repackaging of Jude's Christmas novellas and short stories.

Victorian books

Never Kiss a Toad (with Mariana Gabrielle)
Caught together in her father's bed, Sally and Toad are wrenched apart, to endure years of separation. But neither distance nor malice can destroy true love.

God Help Ye, Merry Gentleman (with Mariana Gabrielle)
In this prequel novelette to *Never Kiss a Toad*, Sally wants to discuss The Scrapbook, a collection of forbidden materials Toad has been sending her. Will Toad survive Christmas?

Forged in Fire (novella in the Bluestocking Belles collection *Never Too Late*)
Burned in their youth, neither Tad nor Lottie expected to feel the fires of love. Until the inferno of a volcanic eruption sears away the lies of the past and frees them to forge a new future.

Contemporary books

A Family Christmas (novella in the Authors of Main Street collection *Christmas Babies on Mainstreet*)
She's hiding out. He's coming home. And there'll be storms for Christmas.

Post-apocalyptic fiction

A Midwinter's Tale (novella in the Speakeasy Scribes collection *Resist and Rejoice*)
Verity Marchand is an orphan of time, her family tavern under the ice that grips Boston. When Verity's dreams lead her into a nightmare, she'll need a miracle—or the family cat—to save her.